BLOOD COLD

A CHRIS BLACK ADVENTURE

The Chris Black Adventure Series

By James Lindholm

BLOOD COLD

A CHRIS BLACK ADVENTURE

JAMES LINDHOLM

CamCat
Books

CamCat Publishing, LLC
Brentwood, Tennessee 37027
camcatpublishing.com

Hardcover ISBN 9781931540353
Paperback ISBN 9780744300956
Large-Print Paperback ISBN 9780744300284
eBook ISBN 9780744300963
Audiobook ISBN 9780744301502

Library of Congress Cataloguing-in-Publication
Control Number: 2020935482

Cover design by Jerry Todd. Book design by Maryann Appel.
5   3   1   2   4

For Zibbo.

Because it's in the suitcase.

Too late. The next swell rolled in, an amorphous blue-green predator stalking its prey. It reached the boy and effortlessly lifted him off the rocks, drawing him back into the water. He quickly disappeared below the surface.

The man screamed, but Chris couldn't hear what he said.

Chris removed his smartphone and wallet, placing them safely in a crack in the rock behind him. The kid was going to be history if someone didn't get to him very soon. He turned to and prepared to make the 10-foot drop, waiting for the next surge of water and trying to keep his eyes on the boy, who was back at the surface for the moment and struggling.

The next swell came and Chris leapt, feet first and shoes on. There were too many dangers beneath the surface to enter head first, and though shoes would make swimming more difficult, against the rocks they would be invaluable.

He hit the water and immediately opened his arms into a T position to halt his momentum and to keep himself at the surface. The frigid water instantly closed around his chest, drawing away his breath.

Chris knew that the 55-degree water, though cold, was not the most immediate problem. Though water wicked away body heat at more than

32 times faster than air, he planned to be out of the water well before hypothermia had a chance to set in. The real threat came from being right in the impact zone as the swells from the north Pacific came crashing in against the barnacle-encrusted rocks.

Two quick overhand strokes got Chris over to the boy. The boy's eyes were wide with panic and his lips were already turning blue. Chris grabbed him with his left arm while trying to get purchase on the rocks with his right.

"It's okay, big guy. I've got you. Let's get you out of here."

1

Bile, mixed with the remnants of some distant meal, erupted from Michael de Klerk's mouth as he was wrenched back into consciousness. His face slammed into the gritty, non-slip back deck of the small boat on to which he'd been dumped. The rhythmic hum of the twin diesel engines vibrated through the thin, vomit-covered deck plates, and de Klerk could feel the boat steaming quickly over the undulating swells. With every third or fourth swell, his body lifted off the deck and hovered briefly before the Earth's gravity drew him back into its massive embrace.

Relief that he was awake swept over him for about ten seconds, but that feeling was quickly replaced by pain, then fright, and then a mixture of the two. In addition to the scratches on de Klerk's face, pain emanated from the back of his head where someone had hit him. There was also the extreme discomfort of his bound limbs—his arms were tied behind his back and, judging from his inability to feel much of his left arm, he had apparently been lying on his left side for quite some time. His ankles were also bound, though this caused less outright agony.

He recalled leaving the office in downtown Cape Town in a hurry; there'd been something important going on, but he couldn't remember what that was. What had he been doing there? He crossed the street to enter the parking structure. Okay. And then he approached his car. Someone must've hit him from behind.

The next thing he knew, he was on this boat. Where was his stuff? His computer?

De Klerk was lying such that his face was directed toward the stern of the boat with his head nestled under the lip of the rear gunwale. He couldn't see anything. As the boat launched off the next swell, de Klerk took advantage of his status to shift his body. When he landed, he was facing toward the cabin of the small boat. The door to the wheelhouse was closed, and he couldn't see over it, so there was no way for him to guess at the number of people inside.

The gradually increasing ambient light around the boat told him it was near dawn, though he couldn't be sure precisely which day was dawning. He could see things more clearly now. There were two five-gallon buckets sitting against the gunwale to his left, each had five or six very large hooks hanging around its perimeter. He thought he could smell an odor of fish coming from the buckets.

Though he was a genius with mapping software, de Klerk was not particularly good with introspection. If his mind was busy with a mapping problem, he was happy. But if he was left alone to his thoughts, well, that didn't usually go very well.

The fact that no one had taken even a moment to check on him heightened his belief that he was in big trouble. Valuable hostages would receive good care. People who were not valuable would not. He'd also watched enough American TV shows to know that if the kidnappers let you see their faces, you were "toast." He'd always liked that phrase.

This latter point taxed his young heart when the boat abruptly cut its engines and drifted quietly on the undulating swells. The door of the cabin opened and three large men emerged, none of whom was wearing any kind of mask to obscure his identity.

De Klerk knew he was toast.

The men wore knee-high rubber boots under Farmer John foul-weather pants. Each sported a sweater of some kind, and all donned knit hats. Only one of his captors looked at de Klerk before joining the other two at the boat's rail. There'd been no compassion in that glance. The other two were pointing at something away to the right and nodding their heads. No one said anything.

That is not to say that it was quiet. The aural void produced by cutting the boat's engines had been filled rapidly with what sounded like a loud cocktail party. De Klerk could hear hundreds or more voices arguing loudly. Overhead, dozens of common seagulls soared, and a penetrating stench was coming from a source de Klerk could not see. The pieces of this puzzle did not fit together well, and he did not understand what was happening.

The men conferred among themselves for a moment, and then two of them began working with the hooks. They each carefully strung three of the large hooks on a line. Next, they reached into the bucket and baited each of the hooks with a large fish head. With all six of the hooks baited, the men tied the lines off at either side of the stern and threw the heads into the water.

Perplexed by this activity, de Klerk's anxiety was temporarily abated as he tried to figure out what these men were doing.

The blue-eyed man came over to him. He squatted down, resting his large arms on his even larger thighs. When he exhaled, his breath smelled of bologna and old cheese.

"Well now, my little friend, you didn't honor our deal and now it doesn't look too good for you. Nope. Not too good at all." He shook his head in a world-weary way that almost made de Klerk believe that the man was on his side, that he didn't want to do whatever it was that he was going to do.

"Please. Please!" de Klerk exclaimed, now in a full-blown panic. "I don't know who you are and I won't say anything. I promise. Please just don't hurt me." He was crying now.

"Now, now. Don't make this any harder than it has to be, my little friend. We are just being paid to do a job, right? We have families, too, right? Won't do for us to come back without having done our jobs, right?"

"Just let me off somewhere and I'll disappear. I'll never tell anyone what happened," de Klerk begged.

"Did you hear that, boys?" the man said, looking back over his shoulders. "He wants to be dropped off somewhere!"

Looking back at de Klerk, the man said, "We can do that, my little friend. We can do that." His tone gave de Klerk no confidence.

One of the other men extracted a coil of line from a compartment in the starboard gunwale. At one end of the line there was a carabiner and a large Styrofoam float.

De Klerk was not a good swimmer. If they were going to put him in the water with his hands tied, he might drown.

"Please. Please don't put me in the water. I can't swim! I'll give all the money back! I will do anything. Please." He paused. "At least cut my legs free. Please!"

The blue-eyed man grabbed de Klerk by his two wrists and hefted him up on to the stern gunwale. Momentarily disoriented by the move, it took de Klerk several seconds to get his bearings.

He was seated on the stern with his legs dangling over the back of the gunwale. In front of him, perhaps seventy-five feet away, was a very small island. More like a large rock pile than a proper island. It was covered with what looked like some kind of seals. There were literally thousands of them. The din of sound that earlier had reminded him of a party was their near-continuous vocalizations, kind of a barking yelp. The stench, even at this distance, was overwhelming.

Seals were coming and going from the island; leaping off the rocks into the water and jumping about in small groups. A small huddle of penguins watched from the water's edge.

A new panic erupted in de Klerk, a panic like nothing he'd ever experienced before. He shook violently and tried to rock his way back into the boat. Large hands clasped down on both his shoulders and prevented him from moving.

He knew he was staring out at Seal Island, a small rocky outcrop located a few kilometers offshore in False Bay. It was known to Cape Town residents, as well as much of the TV-watching world, as the home of South Africa's famous "flying" great white sharks.

De Klerk's mind involuntarily reviewed the last nature special he had seen on TV. This was the spot where one-ton sharks literally leapt from the water at 25 mph in pursuit of their Cape fur seal prey, a behavior rarely seen elsewhere in the world. Erupting from the water, the sharks would split the small fur seals in half. They would then thrash about at the surface in a frothy red mix of seal blood and seawater as they finished off the meal. Sea birds would swarm on the kill spot, grabbing loose seal innards and fighting over them in the air above as the shark thrashed about below. Occasionally, an unlucky seabird would stray too close to the gaping maw of the white shark and become dessert to an already satisfying meal.

Perhaps the most disturbing aspect of these predatory attacks from de Klerk's perspective was the incredible speed with which they took place. If you sneezed, you missed it.

De Klerk knew from his job at the National Marine Research Institute (NAMARI) that the ecotourism industry that grew up around the breaching sharks followed a simple daily routine guaranteed to satisfy the curiosity of even the most jaded traveler. Arrive on site at Seal Island at sunrise to watch the natural acts of predation, sometimes as many as five events in the first hour. Next, deploy the fur seal decoy on a line from the stern of the boat and motor slowly back and forth just offshore of the island. During the peak of the "shark season" the decoys might produce several instances of shark breaching immediately behind the boat where even the cheapest of cameras took compelling photos.

Finally, the cage would go in the water, along with large fish heads to attract the sharks right to the boat. Here the tourists, many of whom had never worn a face mask or breathed from a SCUBA regulator, not to mention enter the water with a large carnivore, would gleefully enter the cage for a chance to see the prehistoric behemoths swim past, sometimes mere inches away.

De Klerk recalled the talking head on TV say several times that the frequency and intensity of the attacks left one indelible impression on observers, either on-site or thousands of miles away in front of a TV screen—to enter the water at Seal Island outside of a cage meant certain death.

One of the fishermen tugged on a line drifting down current behind the boat. As the man pulled the line, the fish head anchored at its end rose to view, skipping along the surface. Several feet beyond, a large dorsal fin emerged, water streaming to either side as its forward momentum increased.

De Klerk inadvertently evacuated his bowels into his pants as the shark's jaws closed around the fish head only inches below his dangling feet. Tearing the fish head from the hook, the shark violently beat its tailfin against the stern of the boat, drenching de Klerk, then disappearing into the depths. The magnitude of de Klerk's predicament had triggered some kind of deeply rooted self-preservation mechanism. Nothing scared him more at that second than the prospect of being eaten alive by a wild animal. His mind rapidly traveled to another place, a place far away from the hideous reality of his current circumstances.

The small remaining portion of de Klerk's brain that had stayed behind to maintain basic functions listened to the surrounding sounds. "We will end this quickly my little friend if you tell us who else knows about our transaction," one of his captors said. "You were paid a large sum of money for those maps and told not to discuss it. But we know that in fact, you did discuss it. Tell us whom you told, and what you told them, and we will not put you in the water with the fishies. Tell us that, and this will all end. That's a pretty good deal, right?"

Unfortunately, de Klerk was able neither to process nor vocalize anything beyond the guttural moan that was triggered when the first dorsal fin had become visible near the boat. Now several sharks were investigating the fish heads trailing just off the stern.

"That's it? Okay, then," said the man with something like glee in his voice.

Michael de Klerk was tossed over the stern into the fifty-degree water, a line attached to the ropes binding his wrists. The shock of the chilly water was lost on his remnant brain as a few remaining synapses fired. His eyes processed the deep green water below, punctuated by beams of sunlight striking at sharp angles to the surface that would have been beautiful under other circumstances. They observed, too, a large grey shape swim past directly below him.

In a final twist of fate, Michael de Klerk made one last effort to preserve himself with a desperate lunge to the surface for air. That lunge drew the attention of one of Seal Island's larger denizens, a fourteen-foot-long female shark, and in a matter of seconds de Klerk's torso was permanently separated from its lower extremities, relieving the few remaining grey cells in his brain from any further obligations.

2

Extreme danger in nature often accompanies great beauty. Oleander, coral snakes, and even lionfish are enjoyable to behold right up until they poison, bite, or sting someone.

One has to be careful, Dr. Chris Black mused, as he sat along the seawall in the small coastal town of Muizenberg and stared out into the aquamarine surf breaking along the white sand beach. He'd only been in South Africa a week, surfing when he could in between recovering from jet lag and integrating himself into a new research project. He'd travelled many places around the world, but somehow the combination of flights and long layovers for his trip to Cape Town had taken him nearly thirty-six hours.

Since he'd arrived they'd already counted four white shark sightings right here at the main beach. In fact, within two hours after he left the surf the day before, an angler had caught a ten-foot white shark in three and a half feet of water.

That's basically on shore, for God's sake, Chris thought.

Coming from California, where white sharks were always around but attacks were fairly rare, Chris had appreciated from the moment that he stepped off the plane that he wasn't in Kansas anymore. As a scientist, Chris was not prone to anthropomorphisms or sensational news coverage, but he had to admit that South African sharks didn't mess around. They didn't taste you or mistake you for some other more palatable food source. No, they came to dine, and if they got you, you were history. Toast.

Chris had toyed with the idea of a commercial shark dive near Seal Island the previous week but had been discouraged by his South African colleagues, who were not very pleased with the tour operators. He understood the underlying tension between scientists seeking to understand natural phenomena and the ecotourism operations that dramatized the same phenomena to make money. But Chris hoped to get a chance to try it at some point nonetheless. He thought it would be a pity to come all the way to South Africa and not spend some time in the water with white sharks.

To his left, Chris saw a large sign depicting the elaborate flag system that Cape Town had erected at many of the more active beaches to gauge the threat of a shark attack. Paid shark spotters were on a hill above the beach. These keen-eyed citizens maintained a near-continuous watch on the water. That was, Chris assumed, unless they were eating a sandwich or texting someone, in which case all bets were off. Anyway, they operated a straightforward system of color-coded communication to keep the populace informed about the odds of having their legs bitten off.

A green flag meant "all clear," go surfing in your meat suit with reckless abandon. A black flag meant "viewing conditions were poor," or, again, don't believe anything we say because we are eating our sandwiches. A red flag indicated a "high shark alert," which Chris assumed would be flown fairly frequently if for no other reason than to justify the employment of the shark spotters. And finally, there was the white flag. If you see a white flag, run like hell and don't stop until the parking lot because something big is coming after you.

Chris's enjoyment of his own witty insights was interrupted by the arrival of his mother, Dr. Margaret Black, and her "friend," Steven Larsen, who was also a doctor. They came bearing chocolate-filled croissants and freshly squeezed orange juice from a café across the street.

"Seen anything resembling a dorsal fin so far?" Steven asked, handing Chris a croissant.

"Nope, but that doesn't mean much," Chris replied, chomping the end of the croissant with predatory efficiency.

"A man in the bakery told us that white sharks are washing up on shore with their internal organs removed," Margaret said. "He says that Orcas are doing it. Have you ever heard of that before? I don't recall ever seeing anything like that back home."

"From what I've heard, the guy in the bakery may be right on," Chris said. "There've been several documented cases of precisely that. But not today. Nothing's happening other than this guy down here picking up kelp along the shoreline." He gestured to a black man who had spent the past forty-five minutes piling up the kelp along the shore in little piles, assumedly for removal.

"I read about this last night," Margaret said. "Since the end of Apartheid, there has been a major effort to employ as many black people as possible to help enable them in a way that wasn't possible previously." She sat down next to her son.

"When we went grocery shopping last night, there was a man responsible for putting barcode stickers on each of the apples we purchased. When we went out to our car, which had been parallel parked on the street, we paid a few rand to a man who was responsible for watching that portion of the street to prevent burglaries. And I believe that man over there is being paid to remove the unsightly kelp from the beach. It's actually quite extraordinary."

"I know what you mean," agreed Chris. "I didn't understand the stickers when I first went grocery shopping after I arrived. Showing up at the cash register with no stickers created quite a scene."

"It is hard to believe," Steven said, sweeping his hands to the left and the right, "that a country with this exceptional natural beauty was governed by such a backward regime for such a long time."

Chris sat back and enjoyed his breakfast as he took in his surroundings and listened to his mother and Steven discuss the finer points of modern governance. He weighed bringing up the current occupant of the White House, and the utter havoc the guy had wrought on the country in general, and on science in particular. The beauty and potential of a country did not always go hand in hand with smart or even merely competent governance. But he decided to save that endless conversation for another less relaxing moment.

Chris was the assistant director of the university's Center for Marine Exploration (CMEx) in Central California. He was a marine ecologist with a long track record of conducting successful field research at locations around the world. In his fifteen-year career he'd done all the things that research scientists were supposed to do: raise grant money, support students, publish scientific papers, and give public presentations. Success in that regard had resulted in the highly sought after professorial tenure at the university two years before and some local notoriety.

But at the same time Chris was much more than just an academic force. He was also a fairly imposing physical presence. At thirty-nine years old he was still in great physical shape. The lines on his face and the grey streaks in his otherwise dark hair only added to his overall charisma, or so he had been told on a couple of occasions. People had also told him that he looked like Agent Mulder from the *X-Files*, but Chris wasn't convinced on that score. However, he was always impressed when anyone mentioned one of his favorite TV shows.

Chris had come to South Africa for a multitude of reasons, only one of which was to participate in a new research project taking place a few miles to the south of where he currently sat, down the west coast of False Bay. Six months ago, back home in California, Chris and his colleagues had inadvertently stumbled upon an illegal dumping operation while in the middle of a research project deep in the submarine canyon just offshore in Carmel Bay. The incredible rampage and bloodshed that erupted following that discovery had been extremely hard on Chris and his research team.

Months passed and Chris had fully recovered from his physical wounds, but the deeper wounds had yet to heal. The events had not been Chris's first interaction with violent criminals. Indeed, he and his colleagues had somehow found themselves facing danger on numerous occasions at locales around the world. But this most recent episode had fatigued Chris spiritually in a way that he'd never experienced before.

Though the person responsible for the carnage had been brought to ultimate justice and Chris had been instrumental in the man's death, closure had eluded Chris thus far. When he woke up one morning several months ago after another nearly sleepless night and realized the extent to which his enthusiasm for his day-to-day responsibilities at the CMEx had waned, he began to look for something different.

To his great relief, that something different came in the form of an offer from a South African colleague to come down to dive in one of the country's oldest marine protected areas. A six-month research project on a separate continent, about as far away from Carmel as you could go and still be on the planet Earth, was just what the doctor ordered. It was different enough to provide a welcome relief, but it was still consistent with his expertise and training. Though he was prepared to wait tables again if he'd had to, this was preferable by far.

Chris had applied for, and received, a six-month sabbatical from the university to come down here to Cape Town. He knew that the unprecedented speed with which his application had been processed and accepted was largely attributable to the support of Peter Lloyd, his friend and the director of the CMEx. Peter leaned on a few key administrators the way only Peter could lean. Then he'd sent Chris on his way knowing that his best chance to guarantee Chris's continued involvement with the CMEx hinged on giving him a chance to recover his enthusiasm for the job.

The violence of last summer had also touched his mother, Margaret. She was a child psychologist with a successful practice in Carmel. The death of one of her former patients had set events in motion. Margaret had also come very close to being kidnapped at gunpoint by one of the thugs involved in the incident, but Chris had intervened to save her.

Margaret had been watching Chris closely following those events, and he knew she was still worried about him. Though he was sure he'd be fine eventually, Chris was touched by Margaret's desire to travel down to South Africa for the first two weeks of his stay. Steven, Margaret's new friend, had come along as well. And much to his surprise, Chris was actually enjoying his presence.

"Chris. Chris, are you listening?" Margaret asked.

"Er, um, yes. Fascinating point, actually."

"You think that our needing to go look for a restroom is a fascinating point? You are so full of c-r-a-p!"

The shark flag was still green. Chris wondered where he might find a meat suit.

3

By mid-morning Margaret and Steven had left to explore Table Mountain, one of the defining natural attributes of Cape Town. Chris had yet to go up the mountain, though he reflected on it frequently. Its sharp ascent into the sky was much more compelling than a simple mountain. And it reminded him of the feature Richard Dreyfuss carved out of mashed potatoes in *Close Encounters of the Third Kind*.

Chris had piled his SCUBA gear into the back of his newly purchased, but not new, mini-SUV. The gear filled the limited space to capacity.

Chris had learned quickly upon arrival in South Africa that one didn't leave anything in one's car, visible or not. The threat of theft was still ubiquitous, whether a car was parked on the street or behind a gated fence. This was tough for Chris given that he'd had a habit of leaving gear in his truck for most of his adult life, and it was a pain in the ass to continuously load and unload a pile of SCUBA gear. But he resigned himself to overcome.

He was due in Simon's Town in about thirty minutes to catch a boat to the dive site. His friend Daniel had called to remind Chris of the time but wouldn't get off the phone until he'd reviewed several of Chris's near misses in traffic circles over the past week.

"To the left, Chris. The *left*. I know your brilliant scientific mind is busy contemplating the big questions of the universe, but I don't know how much longer I can hold off the local police from chasing you down if we have another incident at the rotary." In his haste to get around his new surroundings, Chris had possibly turned the wrong way on a couple of occasions, irritating some of Simon's Town's citizens.

Daniel Opperman was the marine operations director for the Ark Rock marine protected area. He was perhaps ten years older than Chris and about two inches taller. Chris noted upon arrival that Daniel's skin had achieved the type of deep tan only possible from decades at sea. His blue eyes, when not shielded from the sun by dark glasses, didn't miss anything.

The Ark Rock marine protected area, much like nature reserves on land, excluded any form of commercial or recreational fishing but did allow less impactful activities like sailing and SCUBA diving. It had been in existence since the Apartheid years, and as a result, it generally contained more and bigger fish than the surrounding fishable areas. Chris also knew that the reserve's distance from shore deterred a lot of casual users who might have been more active in the reserve had it been closer to land, providing another measure of protection.

A native of Cape Town, Daniel was the first and only operations director at the reserve. He oversaw the small fleet of boats dedicated to the reserve and served as the primary point of contact for any researchers wishing to conduct scientific studies there. He had called Chris two months earlier to see if he could get any insights into how to best monitor the fish populations in the reserve on a very limited budget. Daniel was surprised, but pleased, when Chris had volunteered to come down to help personally.

With minutes to spare, Chris loaded his gear onto the boat alongside the other two divers working at the reserve, Mbeke Tonobu and Kara

McDonnell. The trio had been diving together for the past week while Daniel operated the boat and kept an eye on things from the surface.

Steaming out to the dive site at barely nine knots while sitting on an uncomfortable bench and listening to the deafening engine noise of the converted fishing vessel, Chris longed for the comforts of the R/V *MacGreggor* back home in California. The *MacGreggor* had been built to conduct marine science and was equipped for the job like no vessel Chris had ever seen. The R/V *Dolores Marie*, on the other hand, had been built for fishing long ago. It had found its way to the reserve the previous year at an auction. She wasn't the *MacGreggor*, Chris mused, but she wasn't without her charms.

Two of those charms came in the form of the two feral cats that had moved onto the boat one day several months ago. As much as Daniel complained about them, it was pretty clear to Chris and everyone else on board that he secretly enjoyed having them on the boat. They both got seasick from time to time, which Chris could have lived without, but he still thought that they had character. He recalled the trip two days before on which he'd taken a nap on the back deck after a long day on the boat. Resting in the sun and out of the wind had been too relaxing an opportunity to pass up. He'd awakened to find the cat called Princess sitting comfortably on his chest, staring at him intently. They had ended up relaxing in the sun together for several minutes. Fortunately, there'd been no sea sickness incidents for Princess while she sat on him.

Chris felt the engines slowing, but quickly noticed that they had not yet arrived at the site. Climbing up the ladder to the fly bridge, he found Daniel on the radio.

"Repeat, vessel leaving the Ark Rock Marine Protected Area. Please reply. You are in a restricted area. Over." Daniel spoke English with an Afrikaner accent, which itself derived from Dutch. His massive forearms stuck out from a red university sweatshirt that Chris had brought him as a gift. The sweatshirt was at least one size too small.

"What's up?" Chris asked.

"I've heard from our enforcement team that there's been some unauthorized vessel traffic in the reserve the past couple of days," Daniel replied. "Unfortunately, none of our boats are fast enough to catch up with the violators."

"Are you thinking poaching?" Chris used binoculars to observe the boat quickly motoring away from them. It was a small boat, perhaps thirty feet in length. He could see three or four people on the stern, one of whom was looking back at him. "I don't see any fishing poles, but they've got a dive ladder off the stern."

"Most likely, my friend," Daniel replied, shaking his head slowly. "We just don't have enough people on the water to protect this place the way it should be protected."

"Was that always the case?"

"What do you mean? Apartheid?" asked Daniel, his eyes forward. "I don't know. To tell you the truth, I think we did have more money for some things, but it was a bad, bad time, nonetheless."

"I've read papers that argue totalitarian regimes are good for the environment," said Chris. "But that is obviously a dramatic oversimplification."

Daniel quietly steered the vessel. This was the most the two men had talked about Apartheid since Chris's arrival. Knowing that they didn't have to get to the bottom of everything right away, Chris moved on.

"Where would they sell their catch?" Chris lowered the binoculars. He thought he might have seen one of the guys holding a rifle before, but it was difficult to confirm at this distance.

"It would not be hard to find a buyer, I'm afraid," Daniel said. "We are not nearly as advanced as the U.S. is in enforcement."

"Oh, you'd be surprised." Chris recalled state and federal budget problems back home that left very little money for adequate enforcement. He'd spent several years working at an island offshore of Santa Barbara. There *was* a ranger station high up on a cliff overlooking the reserve at the island, one of the oldest in California. However, if the single ranger who occupied the station actually saw someone poaching, he'd have to lower his inflatable boat about twenty meters down the cliff using an old mechanical winch. Chris was told that generally by the time the ranger lowered the boat and climbed down the one thousand steps to the water to get in the boat, the offenders were long gone.

"I'll go down and get ready to dive," he continued. Before climbing down, Chris watched Kara and Mbeke preparing their gear on the back deck. Kara was laughing out loud, but Mbeke was quiet. He turned back to Daniel and asked, "Is it my imagination or is Mbeke not a big talker?"

"Ah, you noticed," Daniel replied. "I find that he has a lot to say, usually with Kara around, but he is very careful with his words most of the time. I think at some point during his time at university he was hassled by other kids about his accent. Not everyone was supportive of a young black kid going to college, and they let him know it."

"That's a shame. I bet those kids wouldn't want to mess with him now, though."

Daniel nodded. "That's true."

"Well, there's nothing wrong with being quiet. In fact, if we all said less, we'd probably get along better."

4

"There's someone checking us out with binoculars," Pieter Jonker observed over the engine noise as the boat he was on motored away from the reserve.

Jonker was standing on the back deck, still wearing a battered old Farmer John wetsuit from the dive he had just completed, his white-blond hair drying in the sun. His bare arms revealed tattoos extending from his wrists to his well-muscled shoulders, all completed during various periods in prison. Jonker's latest stint behind bars had been in Pollsmoor Prison in Cape Town, which had earned notoriety two decades before for incarcerating Nelson Mandela. Jonker had received three years in the prison for manslaughter after killing a family of four while trying to outrace the police in a stolen sports car. The sentencing judge had remarked, for the record, how much Jonker's blasé attitude about human life appalled him. Jonker had shrugged off the judge's disdain and the relatively short period in prison.

"Looks like it might be that Yank," Jonker added as he moved inside the cabin where the engine noise was significantly reduced.

"They'll never catch us in that tub," Jacob Slovo replied from behind the wheel. Slovo was a middle-aged native of Namibia. His skin was as deeply black as Jonker's hair was white. The visible scars on his face, neck, and arms suggested a life of violence, and his reputation for ruthlessness was widespread. He looked down at Jonker, who stood at least six inches shorter and added, "And I'm not worried about Opperman and that American scientist. Tell me about the dive."

Jonker was born after Apartheid had ended and didn't particularly care that he was reporting to a black man for this latest job. In the end, he thought the potential payoff was more important than anything else. And Greyling must have his reasons for using Slovo.

He watched his dive buddy laboring with their equipment on the back deck while he gave his report to Slovo, "We found the wreck after about fifteen minutes on the bottom. It's not exactly where we figured it would be. It's sitting on the edge of a reef about twenty meters down, and it's covered with growth."

"Growth? What are you talking about, growth?" Slovo had never been underwater. His skills as a river boat driver in Namibia had translated well to boats on the ocean, but he still had no interest in going *under* the water.

"You know, shit all over it man, sponges and plants and stuff. Fishing line. It was covered with that stuff, and a lot of fish as well. We had no bottom time left after those two earlier dives, so I didn't have time to look closely," Jonker said, then added quickly, "But the hold was intact, so the gold should be safe." He had no reason to believe the gold wasn't in the wreck just as Greyling had told him. He didn't understand how Greyling had found out about it, but he'd learned from experience that the old man knew what he was doing.

Years before, while out on a crime spree with several friends he'd known since elementary school, Jonker had inadvertently tried to rob the wrong guy outside of a Cape Town bank. The man, it had turned out, worked for a former government official named Willem Greyling. The robbery had been thwarted and Jonker's gang had escaped. It wasn't until a week later that the gang encountered the man again, this time surrounded by several well-armed friends. That confrontation ended with six of Jonker's eight friends dead and one with a serious, lifelong head injury. Jonker had been left alone but was compelled to come to work for Greyling, or else. Indifferent to whom he worked for, Jonker had taken to his new job and had never looked back.

Slovo was more skeptical about any gold on the wreck. "I'll believe the gold is there when it's on the fuckin' deck, you understand." He glared at Jonker. "Tell me more about the hold."

After years of working for Greyling, Jonker didn't scare easily. But he didn't like being stuck in the small cabin with someone like Slovo. The handle on the machete strapped to Slovo's belt looked like it had seen a lot of use. "The boat is sitting on the bottom in the sand. So many of the wrecks we've been diving on are totally destroyed when we find them. This one isn't. And that's a good sign."

Slovo brought the boat around and headed for port.

"We are going to have to go back tomorrow," he told Jonker. "Tonight, you and Nelson, or whatever the fuck his name is back there, need to shut down Opperman's boat. I don't care what you do; just make sure that boat can't come out tomorrow. You got it?"

"Got it," Jonker said, looking away from the scarred face as quickly as he could. He didn't bring up that he and Nelson, at Greyling's direction, had already messed with the scientists' SCUBA gear. It was a long shot that anything would happen, but if it did, maybe they wouldn't have to worry about sabotaging the boat tomorrow after all.

5

Chris held his gauges and other equipment close to his chest with one hand and his SCUBA regulator in his mouth with the other, and then he rolled backwards over the rail. Though he had upwards of four-thousand SCUBA dives logged to date, he still enjoyed the rush of adrenaline that accompanied entering the water from a boat—the brief plunge through space, the sudden submergence after hitting the water, and the rapid acclimation to breathing underwater.

He popped to the surface briefly and tapped his head with a gloved hand, the universal sign for "I'm okay." Kara handed him his dive slate, and then he looked around for his buddy, Mbeke.

Kara and Mbeke were a study in contrasts. Mbeke was a thirty-year-old graduate student at the University of Cape Town. He had grown up poor in the extensive shanty town along the city's eastern border but through the pure force of will had studied hard and made it to college. Once at the university, Mbeke had blossomed as a scholar and quickly ingratiated himself with key research faculty. Upon graduation he'd been admitted to the Ph.D. program with full financial support from NAMARI. He was working on a doctoral dissertation focused on the potential benefits of marine protected areas for reef fishes in False Bay. And at six foot four inches and two hundred and fifty pounds, he was possibly the largest Ph.D. candidate in South Africa's history.

In contrast, Kara McDonnell was a five-foot-seven-inch blonde woman who was raised in a gated community on the upper slopes above the city. Private schools had prepared her for a life of scholarly pursuit, and her parents had generously paid her way. Though barely one hundred and ten pounds soaking wet, Kara could easily match Mbeke in pure enthusiasm for her work. Chris had enjoyed working with both of them so far.

This was the dive team's third and deepest dive of the day. The first two dives, as planned, focused on surveys of reef fishes in shallower water. Mbeke and Chris took turns counting fish, identifying them, and estimating their sizes. Since she had done four dives the previous day on a separate project, Kara would serve as the back-up diver this time around; she was suited up and ready to go in the event of an emergency.

During the steam out to the site in the morning, while the divers reclined in the sun eating fruit, Daniel had told Chris and Mbeke about a wreck he and Kara had seen on sonar the previous week. The maritime history of False Bay was replete with hundreds of storied wrecks, ranging from the seventeenth century to the present. Some of those wrecks were famous, some infamous, but most were completely lost to history after sinking.

As the manager of the MPA, Daniel had been charged with the conservation and management of both the natural resources as well as the "submerged cultural resources." So he'd been thinking about the newly discovered wreck continuously over the past week. Since both Chris and Mbeke's dive computers had indicated that they had enough bottom time for one dive, the pair had agreed to check out the wreck.

Chris spotted Mbeke waiting for him on the mooring line at the bow and swam over to him. Rather than anchor repeatedly within the reserve, which could easily damage the reefs and other habitats, Daniel had placed mooring lines throughout the reserve with permanent anchors, so that a boat could tie up to a surface float without having to deploy its own anchor.

According to Daniel, the wreck was only fifty feet east of the mooring anchor in sixty feet of water. Chris and Mbeke followed the mooring line down into the deep green water. The visibility was perhaps ten feet, not the worst Chris had ever experienced but certainly not the best, either.

Diving in these conditions required a certain measure of cognitive dissonance—one inherently wants to survive, but at the same time one understands that conditions such as these are frequently optimal for consumption by a large predator. Fortunately, Chris knew from experience that divers were less likely to run afoul of white sharks than was the case with surfers.

They reached the mooring anchor resting on a sand patch among rocky outcroppings and set their compasses for due east. Small fishes were abundant in all directions, but Chris could see larger fish swimming around at the edge of visibility. Since he was new to the area, Chris shadowed Mbeke and let him lead the way.

About five minutes later the wreck appeared out of the gloom, sitting upright in the sand and against the reef. It was covered with invertebrates, so much so that the large anemones and sponges prevented Chris from getting a good look at the vessel itself.

A sudden explosion of air bubbles bursting from behind Mbeke's head drew Chris's attention away from the wreck. He quickly closed the distance to Mbeke to try and see what was going on. Air seemed to be escaping from Mbeke's tank as though the valve had broken off. He didn't understand what could have triggered such a thing but pushed those concerns aside to deal with the problem at hand.

Chris could see the alarm in Mbeke's eyes as no air flowed through his primary regulator. He quickly handed Mbeke the secondary regulator he wore on a smaller, separate tank called a pony bottle that Daniel had asked him to use for the deep dive. Unaccountably, Mbeke's distress only seemed to intensify with the new regulator in his mouth. Quickly Chris realized why. He could see no bubbles being expelled as Mbeke lashed out in terror in an attempt to grab Chris's primary regulator out of his mouth.

With all two hundred and fifty pounds of Mbeke bearing down on him, Chris instinctively dropped to the seafloor to evade Mbeke's grasp, hoping that Mbeke would not want to go any deeper. The plan worked briefly, but then two new problems arose as quickly as the other one was solved. Mbeke was shooting for the surface. And his thrashing attracted the attention of a white shark that now swam into the area to investigate.

6

Chris knew that every SCUBA diver trained within the past thirty years had been taught that rapid ascents to the surface were fraught with peril. If a diver rises in the water column too quickly, a multitude of problems can develop. The compressed air that SCUBA divers breathe includes seventy-eight percent nitrogen, which rather than being metabolized by the body like oxygen, remains dissolved in a diver's bloodstream while he or she is at depth. If a diver ascends too quickly after a long dive, the nitrogen in his or her blood turns back into gas bubbles. Those gas bubbles tend to collect at people's joints, causing great pain and contortions, leading to a condition called the bends. Alternatively, if a diver holds his or her breath while ascending, expanding air bubbles in the lungs might literally break free and travel elsewhere in the body. Known as a gas embolism, this can result in a heart attack or a stroke depending on where the escaped bubbles travel. And yet, Chris knew, the single strongest human impulse when a problem arises underwater is to speed to the surface.

Drawing upon the mantra of his old friend Mac, Chris sought to solve the first problem first, which meant he needed to keep Mbeke from shooting to the surface and to get him some air. The shark would have to wait.

Chris deflated his buoyancy compensator to make himself as heavy as possible and grabbed Mbeke's fin hoping to halt the ascent. It worked. Switching his hand to Mbeke's weight belt, Chris passed Mbeke his own regulator. This type of "buddy breathing" typically required each diver to take two full breaths from the regulator before letting it pass back to the other person.

SCUBA diving depended on the buddy system. Every diver carried a second air source. Sometimes that air source was an extra tank, with its own regulator, but more frequently it was a secondary regulator connected to the diver's main tank. This other regulator or "octopus" as it was commonly referred to, was for use by a dive buddy in the event of trouble. In this case, however, with Mbeke already significantly agitated, Chris chose to hand Mbeke his own regulator hoping that the recognition that Chris had been breathing out of it himself would help to calm Mbeke.

Chris held firm to the regulator's hose as Mbeke took two breaths. By the fourth breath Chris was starting to become concerned he himself would be needing air pretty quickly, but he could also see in Mbeke's eyes that the panic was subsiding. Slowly, but firmly he drew the regulator away from Mbeke to take his own two breaths. He flashed the "okay" sign, hoping to reinforce Mbeke's return to calmness. After several rounds of breathing, Chris noted on his dive computer that his air supply was dwindling quickly. At sixty feet water depth, they would need every last bit of air to make it safely to the surface.

Chris briefly let go of Mbeke's weight belt and signaled him the thumbs up, meaning, "it's time to surface." Mbeke replied with the okay sign and they both began to kick up from the seafloor.

The challenge now was to ascend together and slowly, which Chris knew from dozens of rescue training dives over the years, was easier said than done. Prevented from looking at his dive computer while he buddy-breathed with Mbeke, Chris focused on the bubbles they each exhaled. A simple rule of thumb for surfacing from a SCUBA dive was to ascend slower than your bubbles. It wasn't a failsafe way to avoid an air embolism, but it would have to do.

The pair had made it about fifteen feet off the bottom when Chris simultaneously saw Mbeke's eyes bulge in fear as he felt the pressure wave behind him. He couldn't see but sensed the white shark swimming by. He glanced to his right while Mbeke took his breaths and looked right into the beast's large black eye. It took the animal several seconds to pass. Chris judged its size to be close to fifteen feet. The powerful surge of its tailfin gently rocked the pair.

She's coming back, Chris thought. He'd seen no claspers near the anal vent when the shark came past, so he knew it was a female. He also knew that she would most likely be back for another look. White sharks were generally weary predators and liked to look things over before striking.

Years ago, Chris had been diving at Point Lobos back in Carmel to replace one of the team's many acoustic receivers deployed in the area. The receivers were essentially "listening stations" that were anchored to the seafloor to listen for acoustic transmitters that Chris and his colleagues had implanted in fish. If a fish with a transmitter swam into the range of a receiver, its presence was recorded. With dozens of receivers deployed around the area, the movement of a tagged fish could be monitored for years at a time. And understanding where fish moved helped managers to protect them more efficiently.

Each receiver needed to be recovered from the seafloor every three months to avoid filling up its memory card. That meant a lot of very short dives. Three minutes to get to the bottom and find the receiver, one to two minutes to swap it out with a new one, and three to four minutes to get back to the surface.

It was on one of these dives that Chris had first encountered a large white shark swimming right at him. He'd been using a battery powered scooter to move around quickly underwater, and he assumed that this was what had probably first attracted the shark. Seeing the shark swimming right at him, mouth open, Chris had turned off the scooter and dropped four feet to the seafloor. That act had startled the shark and it had turned around.

However, seconds later it was back. This time, Chris was lying flat on the bottom and not moving. He knew that sharks normally preyed upon animals at the surface, and he'd hoped this would deter an attack. It had worked. The shark had come right at him again, but it had appeared no longer interested in him. He recalled feeling numb as the shark swam over right over him and moved off into the green water.

Chris and Mbeke made it another thirty feet toward the surface before the shark returned. This time she advanced slowly from behind Mbeke and Chris watched her entire approach. He turned Mbeke a bit and stared right at the shark, hoping that direct eye contact served as a deterrent to an attack. She moved past, but her moves were less fluid than they'd been before. Chris feared she was becoming agitated. If that were true, the next time they saw her she would be coming fast from below, and it would be too late.

It was clear to Chris that Mbeke was very tense. His rate of breathing had increased and his grip on the regulator was more and more firm. Chris dumped some air out of his buoyancy compensator vest to slow their ascent and he tried to motion to Mbeke to do the same thing. Boyles' law dictated that a given volume of air would increase in volume as it was released from pressure. That meant that any air that either diver pumped into their vests when they were on the seafloor would increase in volume dramatically as they moved progressively shallower and the pressure of depth was relieved. That increased volume of air, if not dumped from the vests, would send the divers rocketing to the surface.

Mbeke complied with Chris's suggestion and dumped some of his air. They passed twenty feet, then fifteen. Chris had been concerned that they would run out of air because they were both breathing off the same tank. But it now looked like they would make it to the surface.

As they passed fifteen feet, the depth at which divers normally took a three minute "safety stop" to purge excess nitrogen from their bloodstreams and avoid the 'bends,' Chris motioned to Mbeke that they should continue to the surface. The risks of skipping the safety stop had to be weighed against the likely return of the shark.

As luck would have it, they broke the surface only feet from the rear of the boat. Daniel and Kara were both at the stern ready to help. Daniel came out onto the dive platform mounted at the stern and reached for Mbeke's tank to help him pull it from the water.

"What happened down there?" he asked with concern in his voice. Then, as he noticed the absence of a tank valve on Mbeke's tank he added, "What the hell?"

"Let's talk about that in a second," Chris said, sticking his mask underwater briefly to look for the shark. "Get Mbeke on board."

Mbeke tossed his fins onto the platform and was climbing up the aluminum dive ladder when Kara yelled and pointed, "Chris, shark coming behind you at forty feet!"

Of course there is, Chris thought, as he quickly considered his options. He'd let himself believe that, like the shark in Carmel all those years ago, the shark had departed and that they were done with the drama for this dive.

Back home Chris knew divers who'd logged thousands of dives along the coast of California without ever seeing even a brief glimpse of a white shark. The fact that he'd had two separate interactions with what the Australians called "the landlord" made him a statistical anomaly. In fact, where regular citizens were horrified when they heard the stories of Chris's interactions with sharks, his scientific colleagues had unanimously agreed that they were envious of the opportunity to see the large beasts in person.

Chris understood this perspective, and he would have most likely felt similarly once upon a time. But no more. After a second incident with a shark off Monastery Beach in which a huge shark had hit Chris hard from behind, his attitude about sharks had evolved significantly. In his youth, while surfing with his friends, Chris had frequently proclaimed proudly that he would much rather die in the gaping maw of a large white shark than reach old age. But after a close and personal experience with a gaping maw, he no longer felt that way. Chris now regularly felt himself hoping that old age would be achievable, though sometimes the odds didn't seem that good to him.

With gear and fins still on, climbing the ladder was not going to work for Chris. He could swim to the edge of the platform and hope that Daniel could help pull him on deck, but if that didn't work, he would be a sitting duck.

Kara called out again, "Chris, it's coming fast! Get out of there!"

A plan came to him and he submerged.

"What the hell is he doing?" Daniel asked.

Mbeke lay down on the back deck exhausted. Kara and Daniel instinctively moved off the dive platform to the relative safety behind the gunwale as the dorsal fin approached.

Chris realized his best plan was to use the submerged portion of the dive ladder to his advantage. He swam over to the ladder and pulled himself around to the other side. He could now see the shark coming straight at him through the murky green water just below the surface. Rays of sunlight danced over its scarred body obscuring its shape.

Had Chris not known it was there, he might not have seen the shark at all.

The swells passing under the boat shook and bounced the dive ladder violently, but Chris held fast, pulling his knees up to take full advantage of the small bit of protection the ladder provided. The shark came in fast and attacked the ladder, wrapping its protruded jaws around the middle rung. Chris saw a tooth break off and spiral slowly into the depths. As the shark moved to the left, Chris moved too, keeping the ladder in between himself and the large fish. It quickly circled and rushed forward again, but appeared wearier this time and did not strike at the ladder.

Sensing an opportunity, Chris removed his fins, sticking his arms through the straps so that he could hold onto them but still use both his hands. When the shark moved again under the boat, he climbed the three steps to the dive platform in short order and sprawled out next to Mbeke on the back deck.

"And I wasn't even wearing my meat suit," Chris said.

"What?" Daniel asked, looking to Kara for an explanation.

"Don't look at me, I have no idea what he's talking about."

Chris continued, "Well, I guess I won't have to go on that shark tour after all. I just saved $150! What is that in rand?"

7

"Reporters are here and they want to talk to you," Daniel told Chris as he walked back into his office. There was a weary smile on his face. "They're down the hall in the main conference room speaking with Kathryn. I think she must have called them after your adventure with that little fish yesterday. What is it that you Yanks say? 'No such thing as bad press?'"

Reposed on Daniel's unusually comfortable office couch, hands behind his head, Chris just grunted. He'd been awake since about 4:00 a.m. that morning, and he was tired.

On the plus side, however, the international selection of movies on *Netflix* had some interesting choices not available back in the States.

"Come on," Daniel continued, undeterred in his apparent mirth. "You're a Yank scientist who almost got himself chomped. That's big news around here. Just go down there and show them your pretty face, and then we can get on with business."

"Maybe I'll tell them you saved *my* life and point them down here," Chris replied as he peeled himself off the couch, smiling at the gallows humor that was common to field scientists worldwide and locking it away for future retribution.

Daniel lowered his voice an octave and said, "Seriously man, I haven't had the chance to talk to you about yesterday. Mbeke told me what happened under water. He says he panicked while you stayed calm. Buddy in trouble, shark circling . . ." He shook his head slowly.

"I talked to Peter Lloyd back in California just to let him know that you are okay. He had a lot to say, but the upshot was that you are 'the man' when things get rough. I think he used the term 'cool customer' more than once."

"Well, don't get too excited. I think Peter just likes saying 'cool customer.' And Mbeke did fine. None of our training really prepares us for valves coming off tanks underwater, or having that happen when large predators are circling," Chris replied over his shoulder as he headed out the door and down the hallway to Kathryn's office.

Kathryn Wekesa, the Directory of NAMARI, was standing to his left under the bright lights of the camera crew. The main camera man towered over her, but she seemed undeterred. At five and a half feet and an easy one hundred and ninety pounds, she was almost as wide as she was tall. Her still-dark hair was shoulder length, and her face held wrinkles both on her brow, from thinking, as well as around the upper edges of her mouth, from smiling. She wore a silver chain on her glasses, affecting the appearance of a high school librarian. In the short time that Chris had been working at NAMARI, he had learned that people underestimated Kathryn at their peril. She hadn't become the director through charm alone. She was tough—as any black woman in South African society had to be.

"Ah . . . Chris, there you are," Kathryn said, breaking from whatever she had been talking about on camera, her eyes on him. "This is Dr. Chris Black from California." She turned back to the cameras. "He's here working with us on the development of monitoring protocols for the Ark Rock Marine protected area. Come on over and let me introduce you."

Chris approached slowly as the reporter and camera woman turned his direction. He'd done his fair share of interviews over the years, some noteworthy, some less so. He'd learned that he was more comfortable talking science than he was about other exploits, which made him nervous about this interview.

The male reporter had a weak, strangely moist handshake that summoned images of hagfish—a.k.a. slime eels—for Chris. The ill-fitting grey suit completed the picture. Nothing like an underwhelming introduction to get your subject talking, he thought. Wresting his hand from the hagfish, Chris was relieved to get a solid shake from the young woman operating the second camera.

He tried to convey sympathy for her as he shook her hand, and he humored himself with the thought that she had received the message loud and clear.

"Mr. Black, uh . . ." the hagfish began.

"That's Doctor Black," Kathryn interrupted.

"Yes. Well, right. *Doctor* Black," the hagfish continued, "would you say that your near miss yesterday underwater resulted more from a general lack of preparation or a lack of familiarity with the local environment? You *are* far from home."

Recalling a principle he'd heard on a political show years ago, Chris chose to reject the premise of the question. "That's a great question. I think the most important thing to remember is . . ."

Back on Daniel's couch after the interview, Chris, Daniel, and Kathryn pondered potential explanations for the incident with Mbeke's tank. Gone was any semblance of humor in Daniel's voice.

"Like I explained to Chris this morning," Daniel said, "those tanks were filled and on the boat the night before our dive. Mbeke filled them all, and I stowed them down in the hold myself. There is just no way that the tank valve should have failed like that . . ."

In the immediate aftermath of the incident it'd been clear that Mbeke's tank valve had literally sheared off the tank, causing his regulators to become detached from their air supply.

"What about inspections?" Kathryn knew that SCUBA tanks require full hydrostatic testing every five years and a visual inspection every year.

". . . *and* I just did visual inspections of all the aluminum 80s last month," Daniel continued in the same breath as if he'd anticipated Kathryn's question.

"What about flaws in manufacturing?" she asked.

"Possibly, but it would be the first time anything like that had happened to a tank under my care." Daniel was holding his head now. "I just don't understand it."

"Okay. So, a tank valve shears off unaccountably while you are at depth. And then the regulator on Chris's pony bottle fails as well." Kathryn looked at Chris. "What are the odds of that happening?"

Daniel adjusted himself in his seat, looking back and forth from Kathryn to Chris. "Two things. First, the manifold inside the second stage of the regulator—the part you breathe out of—was tightened so as not to work at all when under pressure. It worked fine at the surface. But there was no way Mbeke was going to get air out of it like that. It was not that way when I stowed the gear on board the day before. I'm certain of it."

"You tested it at the surface?" Kathryn asked, turning to Chris.

"I did. Nothing more than the standard couple of breaths to make sure that it was functioning, but it seemed fine."

"Daniel, are you suggesting that the gear had been tampered with in some way?" Kathryn asked with a new edge in her voice.

"I guess I am," Daniel replied, now looking at Chris.

"If that's true, there's the obvious question of why," Chris said. "And then there's the fact that not all the gear was tampered with, right?

Other than the pony bottle regulator, the other tanks worked fine for the first two dives yesterday. Weren't you inspecting everything yesterday when I got off the boat?"

Chris could now see the deep bags under Daniel's eyes more clearly than before. He had obviously been up very late.

"That's right. I found no other issues." Daniel nodded.

"So, if we stick with this theory..." Kathryn said to no one in particular.

". . . then someone came on board during the night and sabotaged Mbeke's rig and the pony bottle I was using," Chris finished.

"Well," Kathryn said to Chris, "the reserve, like many in the country, was established under Apartheid. Enforcement at that time was extreme. So there is still a lot of lingering animosity about anything related to Apartheid."

"Our boat is clearly marked as NAMARI," Daniel said, "so we would be an obvious target for someone like that. And security at the dock is not what it used to be."

At that moment, a brown-haired woman stuck her head in Kathryn's door, saw Chris, and said, "Sorry, I didn't realize you had someone with you."

Kathryn said, "That's okay. Chris, this is Claudia Schwarz, one of our biologists. Claudia, this is Dr. Chris Black from California."

"Carmel, to be exact." Chris popped up out of his chair offering his hand. "Nice to meet you."

"Nice to meet you as well," Claudia replied, shaking Chris's hand and looking him in the eyes. "I heard about your experience yesterday. I'm glad everything turned out okay."

"Ah, just happy to be here," Chris said, parroting his close friend Mac's favorite expression in an attempt to get any reply out of his mouth. Claudia had still not let go of Chris's hand, and he was quite fine with that. She looked at him through green eyes.

Chris did not claim to have a comprehensive understanding of human interactions. But he had observed over the years that from time to time he would meet someone and instantly feel some kind of connection; a connection so intense that it was almost palpable. This was one of those times.

Daniel shook his head slowly while Kathryn asked Claudia, "Was there something I can help you with?"

Claudia let go of Chris's hand and replied, "Oh yes, sorry. I was wondering if you've seen MDK at all. I haven't seen him in a couple of days and we were using him to help us with some of our Geographic Information Systems analysis on the fish data."

"MDK?" Kathryn asked.

"Michael de Klerk. Sorry, we all just call him MDK."

"Oh, right. Kara's been his primary supervisor. Have you checked with her?"

"I haven't talked to her in the past couple days while she's been out on the boat," Claudia replied. "I'll follow up with her. Thanks." She then nodded at Chris and walked out of the office.

Kathryn walked over and closed her office door. "Both of you please write up your reports of the incident yesterday, and I'll look at getting some more security down at the dock," she said. "I'm sorry that you have to deal with this Chris. I know that you've been through a lot back home."

Waving off her remark, Chris said, "I really am just happy to be here. Please let me know how I can help."

"One 'cool customer!'" Daniel offered.

"Of all the things I thought I'd be dealing with this week," Kathryn said as she sat back down behind her desk, "sabotage of NAMARI gear was well down on the list. I wonder what's going on."

8

Jacob Slovo watched from the passenger seat as Pieter Jonker turned the ageing 1987 Ford truck from the main highway onto a rapidly upward sloping dirt road. Tall bushes on either side of the road immediately engulfed the truck, and Slovo could see little else.

Slovo didn't like being a passenger. If prison in Namibia had taught him anything, he reminded himself frequently, it was that you had to control your own destiny. If you didn't do that, you either died, or worse, lived to serve the perverted needs of someone stronger.

He'd made it this far avoiding both, and he wanted to keep it that way. His hand instinctively went to the machete strapped to his right thigh. He also didn't like relying on someone like Jonker to get a job done. But then he liked going underwater even less and this job required that, so he'd have to put up with Jonker for now.

Slovo had tried to go underwater once as a teenager. He and his friends had been playing along the shore of the Kunene River in Namibia, trying to keep cool. The river was the place they could avoid listening to their parents arguing at home, while not getting into the trouble the older boys seemed to attract. He recalled that they were all about to go underwater with masks and goggles they'd acquired from different places. His friend Tony was standing in knee-high water wearing a mask, white underwear, and a huge smile as he did a little dance in preparation for going underwater.

Just as Slovo and his two other friends were about to jump in as well, a large Nile crocodile emerged from the water immediately behind Tony, grabbed him by the leg and jerked him under water.

Paralyzed by fear, Slovo stood transfixed only inches from where Tony had been snatched. He watched the ripples radiating from the spot where Tony had been dragged under. Tony hadn't uttered a sound it had happened so quickly. One second he was there, the next he was not. Had his friends not pulled him toward shore, Slovo might have been the crocodile's next meal.

Slovo had never forgotten the look on Tony's face; his eye's bulging in terror behind the old SCUBA mask. And Slovo had never again considered going under water. He'd seen many more crocs during his days driving river boats, but somehow they'd seemed much less menacing from the wheelhouse of a large vessel.

After several minutes, the dirt road levelled out and opened up into what Slovo first took for an abandoned field. To the right he could see old, broken marble statues protruding from the weeds. To the left he noticed what must have been a fountain of some kind, now long overgrown by foliage.

As the truck moved further into the weeds, a single level house became visible ahead. To Slovo it appeared as though the once-fancy house was being reclaimed by the force of nature. The line between yard and house was almost nonexistent, as if something old and irrelevant was erased by the force of everlasting change.

Jonker parked the truck in front of the house and got out without saying anything. Slovo followed him up the now-uneven path to what was left of the front door. Without knocking, Jonker opened the door and beckoned Slovo to follow him. Even though it was midday, very little sun penetrated the dirty and overgrown windows of the house, leaving the interior dominated by long shadows and dark corners.

After his eyes adjusted to the gloom, Slovo saw the old man sitting at a table in front of them smoking a cigarette. The man Slovo knew as Willem Greyling looked like a badly beaten leather suitcase. Deep wrinkles dominated nearly every visible surface. Moist blue eyes peered out from deeply set sockets. The man's grey suit hung loosely on what appeared to be a skeletal frame. Slovo had seen a lot in his life, but there was something different, something eerie about the old man.

It was no secret in South Africa that many of Apartheid's most vicious former officials were still actively exerting influence across the country. In some places that influence was political, but in most it was criminal—from petty crimes to major felonies. With Apartheid gone for nearly three decades, most of its former officials were old—very old—so their only way of exerting influence was bankrolling younger men. Like him. Slovo had wondered where the money to support these criminal enterprises came from, but he assumed it came from long ago embezzled funds.

This particular old man was a legend. Greyling's name had often come up in whispers about human trafficking, slavery and the drug trade. After initial hesitation about getting involved with an old racist, Slovo had decided that he could always kill the bastard once business had been concluded.

"There's my favorite *kaffer*," the old man croaked. They had spoken on the phone twice, but this was their first meeting in person. "Hasn't been a *kaffer* in this house in a long time." He coughed violently and then immediately took another drag on an unfiltered cigarette.

Slovo took several steps toward Greyling. He was not accustomed to being taunted like this.

"You can take your hand off that chopper there, blackie," he continued with effort, as he eyed Slovo's hand gripping the machete with such force that his knuckles turned white. "We're just here to talk. Tell me about the boat."

Slovo briefly peered at Jonker and then back at Greyling. With his eyes now fully adjusted to the dark, Slovo could see what looked like marine charts sitting on the table in from of Greyling. "Why don't you tell me? This is your show."

Greyling coughed again and stared at Slovo. "Very well. My colleagues seem to think that you are important to this operation, so I will indulge them and educate you.

"Years ago, when you *kaffers* took over the government, my colleagues and I sent our money out of the country so you couldn't get your hands on it. Most of that money, all Krugerrands, was put aboard a fishing boat in eighteen plastic barrels. The barrels were placed in the fish hold below decks and the boat was supposed to steam around the Cape and up to Namibia."

Slovo chuckled. "But it never made it."

"That's right, *kaffer*—"

"You better stop calling me that *toppie*," Slovo interrupted as he stepped forward, machete in-hand. To his left he could see Jonker pull a pistol from behind his belt. "And you stay put over there, Jonker, if you want to keep that hand."

Anger flashed in Greyling's eyes and he visibly struggled to sit up straighter, coughing so vehemently that Slovo took two steps back. Greyling paused for a moment then continued, pointing at the marine chart in front of him, "The harbor master's log shows that the boat left here at Kalk Bay at midnight in the middle of a fierce winter storm, supposedly to trawl for hake off the Western Cape. We would have preferred not to send the boat out in the storm, but time was fleeting."

Looking at the map, Slovo could see the Kalk Bay marina where they kept the boat he'd been using for this job. It was just south of Cape Town on the western shore of False Bay.

"The weight of the gold had the boat riding dangerously low in the water," Greyling continued. "Neither the captain, who refused to depart the dock so laden, nor the harbor master, who questioned why the boat was so low in the water before the fishing began, survived the night."

"You killed the captain?" Slovo asked, "With all your gold on board?"

At this point Greyling fell into a coughing fit that lasted two minutes. He reached out with a skeletal hand and wrung a small bell sitting on the table. From the darkness to his left, Slovo saw a young girl carrying a pitcher of water and a dirty glass. She approached the table slowly, without making eye contact with anyone in the room. She left the glass and pitcher on the table and receded back into the darkness. Slovo thought he could smell death wafting up from the path the girl had just taken.

Greyling regained his composure and continued, "Not that it's any of your business, but we judged the first mate more than capable enough to operate the vessel. And there were complications on land that necessitated the boat's quick departure. Despite the storm."

Again pointing to the chart, Greyling said, "Our spotters in Simon's Town, here, reported the boat passing by one hour later, but it was never sighted again."

Looking more closely at the chart, Slovo could see a red, hand-written "X" to the south of Simon's Town where they had been two days ago. "How do you know that your spotters saw *your* boat, *toppie*, and not some other fishing boat?"

"There were no other boats away from the dock that night," Greyling replied. "But that's beside the point. You've already found the boat, had divers on it."

Pointing at the red "X" on the chart with one hand while motioning toward Jonker with the other, Slovo said, "We don't know what we found. Jonker said the hold was intact, but he didn't bring up no gold, *toppie*. Nothing."

Greyling reached out and grabbed Slovo's wrist. Slovo was surprised by the strength of the grip. "I've been kind enough to refrain from terminology you don't appreciate. I expect the same courtesy in return." Greyling let go of Slovo's wrist as he sneered. "I *know* the gold is there, Slovo. I know it. And we are paying you to get it for us."

Massaging the wrist that had turned red from Greyling's grip, Slovo said, "How did you find it after all these years?"

"Two weeks ago, the government sent a research vessel to map the seafloor using sonar." Greyling removed an image from under the nautical chart. "On the second day they came upon our wreck."

Slovo and Jonker both leaned in to better see the image. Neither of them had been given this information before their first trip to the wreck, but both had seen this kind of image before. Sonar was used to produce topographic maps of the seafloor. A computer was used to simulate a light source coming from one direction. The resulting effect was that anything that protruded above the seafloor cast a "shadow." The boat looked to be sitting upright on the seafloor. It appeared to Slovo as though part of the wheelhouse had been torn off, but otherwise the hull appeared undamaged.

Jonker spoke up for the first time, "How did you get a hold of this? We never get to see what NAMARI does."

"We have our sources."

"But if they know about the wreck too," Slovo wondered, "how're we supposed to get the gold with them on top of us?"

"These images were not shared with NAMARI," Greyling replied. "We've seen to that."

"I thought they *collected* the images," said Slovo. "What do you mean they don't have them?"

"Our source is within NAMARI and made sure we had, shall we say, exclusive access to the images."

"And what if your source is convinced otherwise and shares the information with NAMARI after all?" asked Slovo.

"That," Greyling said in a raspy voice that sent chills down Slovo's spine, "is no longer a concern."

"I fear that's where you are wrong, *top*—" Slovo stopped himself just in time. He cleared his throat before he continued. "Jonker will tell you, we saw them out by the wreck a couple of days ago. The government guys and this Yank from California. We slowed them down a bit, but they'll be back."

Greyling sat back in his chair and stared off into the darkness behind Slovo and Jonker. "Looks like one of our sources may not be telling us everything." Turning back to Slovo and Jonker, he hissed. "We *cannot* have government interference! You must make sure that the government does not recover *any* of our gold. Not one single Krugerrand! Go now!"

The man's tone and demeanor were so commanding that Slovo and Jonker almost felt compelled to bow as they left Greyling sitting in the dark.

9

Chris was thirty minutes late to his goodbye dinner with Margaret and Steven at the Kirstenbosch National Botanical Garden. The grounds of the Garden lay at the southeastern edge of Table Mountain in Cape Town.

"There he is!" Margaret leapt out of her chair. "Chris, you made it!"

"Sorry I'm late." Chris approached the table. "It was a near thing."

"Left side of the road?" Steven asked.

"I'm afraid so." Chris shook his head. "Do you remember *A Fish Called Wanda?*"

"Assshoooooole!" said Steven, loud enough to be heard over the din of the crowded restaurant and attract the attention of the neighboring tables.

"Steven! Good heavens. What has gotten into you?" Margaret said with clear exasperation.

"Err, it's a Monty Python thing. Kevin Kline. Left side of the road," Steven said quickly.

"Marvelous. Chris can fend off a big shark, but he can't find the biggest landmark in South Africa. And now you've launched into profane verbal outbursts . . . in public, no less. I wonder what we can look forward to next."

Steven patted Margaret's forearm to placate her, but muttered under his breath, "Just don't call me stupid!" That earned him a high five from Chris and another long, hard look from Margaret.

"Okay, you two idiots," Margaret said. "I was going to skip the Table Mountain facts recitation, but now I don't think I will." Margaret and Steven had done a cable car tour to the top of the mountain earlier in the day.

"Chris, what's the highest point?"

"Uh, two thousand feet?"

"Wrong! A little over thirty-five hundred feet. Steven, what sits at the highest point, and when was it established?"

An hour later, after laughing their way through Table Mountain trivia and ultimately a variety of old stories about Margaret, Steven and Margaret rose to leave.

"Thank you both so much for coming," Chris said. "It has been great these past couple of weeks adjusting to South Africa knowing that the two of you were close by."

"You've been through a lot back home, Chris," Margaret said as she hugged him. "I just want you to have a quiet time down here if that is at all possible. No more sharks."

"I'm sure he'll do his best." Steven patted Chris on the back.

"Just tell me that you're going to be okay," Margaret continued. "I can't leave unless I know that you will be okay."

Chris was not sure what to say under Margaret's penetrating, all-too-knowing glare. He'd thought about this as he drove to dinner earlier that night. Would he be okay? Most likely. Would he be okay soon? Now that was a little less likely. It would take a lot of time to accept that one of his team mates had been killed on his watch, and he might never be able to forgive himself. And losing Abby, although he understood why she had left him, made him want to build a stone wall around is heart.

Not exactly what his mother and other well-meaning souls recommended he should do.

Chris wasn't fond of the self-help genre, and he'd received a great deal of unsolicited advice over the past few months. The best advice that he'd read basically suggested that he should cut himself some slack and give himself room to recover by not creating unreasonable expectations for that recovery. Keeping busy by diving and surfing as much as possible seemed to be the best medicine for him at this point.

He turned and hugged Steven, too, briefly making eye contact with Margaret. "You guys know where you're going?"

"Oh yes," Margaret said. "If Steven learned nothing else from those years at Cambridge, it was how to drive like a local on the left side of the road."

"As long as I have you on the iPad for navigation, we should be fine," Steven said.

"Assshooooooole!" Chris said, noticing a colleague from the nearby University of Cape Town sitting at the bar. "Have a safe flight. Call me when you've had a chance to recover Thig from Peter."

Chris had left his dog, Thigmotaxis, or 'Thig,' a soft-coated wheaten, in the care of Peter Lloyd for the past two weeks. Margaret was to take over after she returned. Though Chris hated the idea of leaving Thig behind, the logistical challenges of bringing her to South Africa were insurmountable. And he knew that she would secretly love staying alternately with both Peter and Margaret anyway.

"Oh, that will be precious," Margaret responded. "But aren't you going to walk out with us?"

"I see a colleague over there from the university. I should touch base with him before I head home."

"Okay. I love you, Chris."

"Love you, too, Mom. Take care, Steven."

10

Margaret and Steven walked out of the restaurant arm in arm into the twilight, the sun having set behind Table Mountain only moments before. Huddled together against the evening chill they slowly meandered through the rows of parked cars in search of a rental they were both convinced was green.

Chris's father, Andrew, had passed away five years before, and Margaret had been in no hurry to meet anyone new. Her work as a counselor for the kids of Carmel kept her busier than most women her age, and she liked it that way. Margaret recalled Andrew as an honorable man, but a tough man to love. And when forced to admit it to herself, she knew that the love had largely left the relationship years before his death. Several people had made the effort to reach out to her over the years, two of them quite valiant efforts, but none had lasted. But somehow things seemed to be working well with Steven, and she was grateful for that. Margaret smiled to herself as she realized how surprised she was that Chris appeared to be enjoying Steven's company, as well.

Their path took them past two men and a woman having a spirited conversation behind an open paneled van. Somehow the van struck Margaret as suspicious, and so she looked a little more closely. The taller of the two Caucasian men wore jeans and a tight-fitting black T-shirt.

His long hair was tied back in a ponytail. The shorter and younger man wore a grey hoodie and baggy black jeans. His head appeared shaved under the hood, but he wore a thick red beard. The heavy-set black woman's hair was cut short.

Finding two men arguing in the presence of the woman made her pause briefly, but she didn't want to get involved and encouraged Steven to walk onward.

"Why don't you fuck off, eh?" the woman barked as Margaret looked at her.

"Sorry, we didn't mean to bother you," Steven said.

"I'll bet."

Margaret and Steven kept walking.

"That's right. You just keep on walking, you old fucks!"

Minutes later Margaret exhaled audibly as they approached their green rental car. Steven opened the passenger side door for Margaret and as she leaned over to climb into the car she said, "This really was a wonderful evening, a wonderful day, even with that little episode back there."

"I completely agree," Steven answered as he prepared to close the door. "Chris is an exceptional young man and watching the two of you together is priceless."

"Oh?"

"Well, take it from me," Steven said, "from someone who's never had kids but who's seen a thousand kids damaged and hurt by extraordinarily caustic parenting. You two have a very good thing going."

"That is a very sweet thing to say." Margaret reached out for Steven's hand. "I think we can safely say that he enjoys your company, as well. Now close this door and let's get out of here."

Margaret smiled to herself as she waited for Steven to come around the other side of the car. It took her a minute to realize that he seemed to be taking an exceptionally long time.

11

"Dr. Mekeleze? It's Chris Black," Chris said as he approached the bar. "We met last week after your seminar on urban planning."

"Chris, of course! So nice to see you. Please sit down and let me buy you a drink. I don't get many marine biologists sitting through my seminars."

Dr. Mekeleze was a prominent architect and urban planner at the University of Cape Town. Chris had happened upon a seminar he gave the previous week and had decided to sit in. As a native of the Californian car culture, where you learned early on in life that without a car you had close to zero independence, Chris found Dr. Mekeleze's talk about walkable towns and cities refreshing.

"Thank you. I'd love to. But you'd better make that drink a water. I'm diving tomorrow."

"Whatever you say, my young friend. Now, you must tell me about this incident I heard about on the news today. Some kind of diving accident?"

As he listened to Dr. Mekeleze, Chris's gaze drifted back toward the table where they'd just finished dinner. The table had yet to be cleared, and there, sitting partly obscured under a pile of napkins, he saw Steven's iPad.

"Please excuse me, Dr. Mekeleze. I've just noticed that my mother and her friend left an electronic device behind. I should run it out to the parking lot to see if I can catch them. I should be right back."

Chris grabbed the iPad and walked out the front door of the restaurant. He wasn't sure where Margaret and Steven had parked, so he struck out into the middle of the large lot, which served both the restaurant as well as the much larger Botanical Garden. Scanning above the hundreds of cars, he could see several people scattered around the lot, but couldn't see Margaret and Steven.

And then he heard a woman scream from somewhere to his immediate left. Turning that direction, he could hear a familiar voice yell out, "Steven, NO!"

Chris started running.

He arrived on the scene just in time to see two men lift Steven off the ground and throw him onto the back window of his mother's rental car. Running at full speed, he was instantly infuriated in a way that Chris knew only came from threats to his family. He grabbed the closest guy to him by the back of his shirt and propelled the man into the space between the rental car and truck parked next to it. The man bounced first off the truck and then the car. Not waiting for the man to recover his balance, Chris then kicked the man's left knee from behind, bashed his face into the large side view mirror extending from the passenger side of the truck, before grabbing the man's shirt again and slamming him into the driver's side window on Margaret's rental car.

"Hang on, Mom!" Chris yelled. "And call the police."

As Chris let go of the man now hanging out of the car window, convinced that he was unconscious, he turned to see the man's hooded friend pull out a buck knife from his back pocket. He was standing behind the trunk of the rental car looking back and forth between Chris and the woman standing on the other side of the car.

This was not the first time that Margaret had been in close proximity to violence, nor was it the first time that Chris had to fight to protect her. Six months ago, back home in Carmel, a man had tried to kidnap his mother from her home. Chris had arrived in time to stop the kidnapping, but there'd been a fight. Margaret had seen Chris break the man's arms, but then he'd asked her to leave the room while Chris's friend Mac had forcibly grilled the man for information. Chris knew that it was only his team mate's later death that had prevented Margaret from pressing him on the earlier incident in her house.

Chris, by his own admission, had spent much of the last six months in a daze. He'd certainly had to fight his way out of some precarious situations in the past, some of them very close calls. But having his entire research team threatened, beaten, and Gretchen killed, had impacted him more acutely than any previous incidents.

Though he hadn't talked much about it with anyone other than his buddy, Mac, Chris was struggling to reconcile his generally calm, professional exterior with the more atavistic impulses that surfaced when his friends and family were threatened.

Unfortunately, he'd thought recently, the list of bad guys who'd learned the hard way that Chris and his friends were not people to be messed with had grown considerably.

Watching the man's eyes closely, rather than the knife, Chris felt that atavism fully taking over now, along with the training he'd once put in with Mac on hand-to-hand combat. In his peripheral vision he could see Steven, a man he had come to care for greatly, lying unconscious on the back of the car, the extent of his injuries unclear.

"Mom, is Steven breathing?"

"I can't tell for certain. He's unconscious!" Margaret cried through the shattered back window. "I can't tell anything more. Help is on the way."

"What's the plan now, smart guy?" Chris asked of the hooded thug, while also looking toward the woman. She had not moved away from his mother's car or pulled a weapon. "If you're coming for me let's get it over with." In the distance he could hear a siren.

"That's your mom in there, huh?" the man responded. "Maybe I'll just cut her first, before I do you."

Chris turned to the woman. "It might be time for you to leave. Neither of your friends is going to be walking out of here."

"Oh, is that right?" she replied with a bravado that wasn't matched by her body language.

"Suit yourself," Chris said as he moved quickly toward the man with the knife. He wanted to get to Steven as fast as possible and he didn't want to give the guy any more time to come up with a strategy.

As Chris approached, the man swung the knife clumsily with his right hand in a broad sweeping arc, just missing Chris's chest. But rather than slash back the opposite direction, the man drew his arm in and attempted a second slash in same direction as the first. And Chris was ready for him.

As the second slash came, Chris shifted to his left to let the man's arm pass in front of him. It did, grazing across Chris's ribcage, easily slicing through his jacket and drawing blood.

Shrugging off the pain Chris grabbed the man's extended forearm with his right hand and simultaneously used the palm of his left hand to hammer the back of man's elbow, hyperextending the joint and breaking it instantly.

The man dropped the knife as he screamed in pain, clutching his disfigured arm with his left hand. Chris brought his foot up in a round-house kick to the man's forehead, sending him sprawling back onto the trunk of the car. He then kicked the knife out of range and briefly checked his own wounds. The cut was broad, extending nearly from one shoulder to the other, but very shallow. He knew he'd been lucky.

As Chris pushed the guy off the trunk in order to check on Steven, he looked over the roof of the car at the woman, who was still standing beside Margaret's window. She hadn't moved to check on either of her colleagues.

"You next?" Chris asked.

"No way, man. You attacked us. That's what I'm telling the cops."

"Okay, good luck with that," Chris said as he took Steven's pulse.

Hearing the woman scream out in pain, Chris looked up to see Margaret's hand reaching out the top of the passenger side window which she must have rolled down amid all the action. In Margaret's hand was a small can of mace, the contents of which she was emptying directly into the woman's face. The woman's agony was clearly illuminated by the flashing lights of the approaching emergency vehicles.

12

The emergency room at Groote Schuur Hospital smelled bad, Chris thought, as all emergency rooms did, a gruesome combination of unspecified wounds and the antiseptic cleansers used to clean up after those wounds. Further, Chris knew from recent experience that hospital trips were rarely made at the best of times, which never helped matters.

Chris sat in the waiting room, waiting. Margaret had been allowed back to see Steven, but he had not. The adrenaline from the attack had largely faded, leaving him tired.

He watched the two policemen now stationed outside the waiting room knowing that he was going to have to talk to a detective eventually. But Chris was far more concerned with Steven's well-being to think about anything else.

The ride in the ambulance had been mercifully quick. Steven had remained unconscious throughout the ride, leaving Margaret and Chris to stare at each other quietly as the paramedic monitored Steven's vitals and bandaged the knife wound across Chris's chest. He knew Margaret was conflicted at these times, torn between disapproval of her son's use of physical force to subdue attackers and the relief that resulted following the end of those attacks.

Margaret's life had, for the most part, been one of quiet, contemplative support of troubled children. She'd trained in the hallowed halls of Wellesley College in New England, where violence was largely an abstraction.

And even though her deceased husband Andrew, Chris's father, had fought in Vietnam and come back changed, that too had been somewhat of an abstraction for Margaret. Not so the night's events. Chris hoped he'd have some time later to talk with her.

Chris's thoughts were interrupted as he saw Daniel and Kathryn approach the two policemen then come in through the door.

"Chris! Are you okay?" Kathryn asked as she surveyed Chris's torn shirt and bandaged chest. "What happened?"

Chris gave them a summary of the encounter in the parking lot and asked how they'd known he was here in the hospital.

Daniel responded, "Dr. Mekeleze called us. He saw you being loaded up in the ambulance and was greatly concerned."

"How is your mother's friend doing?" Kathryn asked.

"I don't know. My mom hasn't come out since they went back about forty-five minutes ago."

The three of them sat in silence. Kathryn checked her iPhone, Daniel read an old magazine, and Chris just tried to stay awake by staring at a fake plant in the corner.

A janitor came through at one point and actually watered the plant, causing Chris to doubt his own sanity.

Margaret came through the door fifteen minutes later. Everyone stood up to meet her.

"He's going to be okay," Margaret said, noticeably relieved. "He's going to have a big headache, and a lot of soreness, but all his cuts are superficial and miraculously there were no broken bones."

Chris closed his eyes, which teared up quickly, and exhaled audibly.

Kathryn introduced herself to Margaret and the two women talked briefly while Daniel steered Chris a few feet away.

"How are you doing, man?" Daniel asked. "This has been quite a week for you."

"I'm alright, thanks," Chris said as he rubbed the tears out of his eyes. "I'm grateful that Steven is going to be okay and mad that I let that little wanker get to me with his knife."

"Yeah, but from what I heard the officers tell Kathryn, the two guys that attacked you are here in the hospital as well, and neither of them is conscious." He paused for a moment. "Do you know what they were after?"

"Not really. It sounds like it was just bad luck that Margaret and Steven encountered them in the parking lot."

"Bad luck, indeed. There are two detectives waiting outside to talk with you."

"Those two guys?" Chris asked, gesturing toward the two standing outside the door.

"No. I think those two were there to make sure you didn't go anywhere. See those other two standing over by the nurses' station? They are the detectives."

Chris stood up and turned toward Margaret. "Mom, I'm going to go talk to those detectives right outside."

Margaret came over to Chris, her eyes watering too, and hugged him hard. "This is becoming quite a habit for us isn't it? I get into trouble and you save me. I don't know what to say."

Chris hugged her back. "You don't have to say anything, mom. You did the saving a million times when I was a kid." He gave her a reassuring smile as he uncurled their embrace. "I'll be back in a few minutes and maybe you can take me in to see Steven, if that is possible."

"I'll make sure that it is," she replied.

Margaret, Kathryn, and Daniel watched as Chris opened the door and walked over to the detectives.

"I've never seen anyone handle trouble as calmly as Chris. He simply doesn't panic," Daniel said.

Margaret looked at Kathryn and Daniel. "As a parent I would love to claim responsibility for that calm, but I can't. Chris has been that way from birth. The French call it *sangfroid*—literally, blood cold."

"I've heard some of the stories, and Chris told me a bit about what happened back in Carmel. It's pretty remarkable stuff. I wouldn't believe it if I didn't know Chris. And Mac Johnson has filled me in on other things, as well. He's not one to exaggerate."

"Oh, it goes much further back than that. I remember a day back when Chris was barely two years old. Andrew and I had set up a play date with the four-year-old that lived next door. It wasn't such a great idea, as it turns out.

"I came out into the back yard after not hearing anything for a couple of minutes. The neighbor was holding our wooden tree swing with both arms above his head. Before I realized what was happening, he let the swing go and it swung down and hit Chris directly in the face.

"He was two years old, mind you, and the neighbor was at least six inches taller than he was at that time. Chris didn't move. He didn't cry. He didn't shout out. He didn't even look away. He just stood there looking at the boy through watering eyes. It was astonishing."

Shaking her head slowly, Margaret continued, "Chris's father was tough. But Chris is something else altogether."

13

Two days later, Chris pushed Steven in a borrowed wheel chair up a ramp toward the gate at the Cape Town International Airport. The bustling terminal was packed with travelers headed off to points around the globe.

Kathryn had arranged for a van to take them to the airport directly from the hospital after Steven's doctor had given him the greenlight to fly home to California.

"If I had a dime for every time I've pushed you up a ramp in a wheelchair . . ." Chris commented above the din of humanity as they approached the gate.

Margaret inhaled sharply. Steven chuckled to himself as he dug for something in his pants pocket. A second later a dime arced through the air towards Chris.

"I guess that should make us square," Steven said.

"I should have said a quarter," Chris said. "You can't buy anything with a dime these days."

The ride to the airport had taken approximately half an hour, giving Chris, Margaret, and Steven time to say their final good-byes.

"Please tell me you're going to be okay, Chris," Margaret said as they approached the gate. "I can't leave you here unless I know that."

Chris smiled. A mother's concern never waivers and rarely diminishes, he reflected. "I'll be fine. Once the two of you leave the country, things will slow down considerably. I'm just going to dive with Daniel and his crew and keep my head down."

"What about Mac? Is he coming down to help?"

"Mac's got his hands full with operations on the *MacGreggor*. In my absence he's had to deal with a variety of new scientists, and it isn't going well. Actually, I'm sure it's going fine. It's just Mac's buoyant personality coming through."

He hugged Margaret one more time and added, "And please don't forget that Facetime call with Thig. I can definitely use some of her unapologetic enthusiasm right about now. And I'm pretty sure that Peter doesn't know how to use his smart phone, so it'll have to happen when Thig"'s with you."

With Margaret and Steven safely on board the plane, Chris left the wheelchair in the hands of an airline employee and started to walk back through the terminal. He thought about Margaret's parting words and knew her concern was well founded. The recent events in Carmel had thrown them all off their respective games. Chris himself was only now, six months later, beginning to have days where the violence and its consequences weren't omnipresent in his mind. While he and Mac didn't discuss it much, Chris was fairly certain that Mac, too, harbored some major pent up animosity related to the events. Even though they'd seen each of the major players meet their ends, the frustration Chris, Mac, and others felt didn't die with them.

For his part, Chris was fairly certain that his response to the two thugs in the parking lot did not occur in a vacuum. With Steven hurt and Margaret threatened, he was sure that he would have reacted under any circumstances. But Chris also knew that the vehemence of his response was amplified by his experiences back home. The Cape Town detectives he'd talked to back at the hospital, not unlike those back in the States, were not entirely pleased with his actions. They'd told him they understood that his actions were taken in self-defense, but they also made sure Chris knew that they weren't happy about the extent of the damage to the two thugs. As far as Chris knew, both of the guys were still in the hospital.

As Chris approached security from the backside, he could see a man standing on the other side watching him. Chris estimated that the man was about five foot eleven with close-cropped, completely gray hair suggesting that he was in his late fifties or early sixties. He wore a dark suit with a white oxford shirt, but no tie. The expression on the man's face was difficult to read around the black Wayfarer sunglasses he was wearing. He didn't strike Chris as a detective.

"Dr. Black? Frank Donagan, U.S. Consulate," said the man with an outstretched hand. "Nice to meet you."

"Donagan? U.S. Consulate?" Chris asked. "Am I being kicked out of the country?"

"No, no. Nothing like that." Donagan flashed a smile. "Well, maybe a little like that. Those two guys you messed up have the local authorities' panties all tied up in knots. Well, not exactly the two guys per se. It's more the fact that a visiting scientist from the U.S. did the messing up."

Chris liked Donagan immediately. "It was self-defense. They put my mother's boyfriend in the hospital and were threatening her next."

"I didn't say *my* panties were in a knot." Donagan held up both of his palms in surrender. "You don't have to convince me. I'm with you. Frankly, I'm impressed that a scientist from California would dispatch two thugs in such a way. Nine times out of ten, a story like that ends up very differently. You deserve a beer, not a deport order." He smiled, then continued. "No, I'm here on my own accord." Donagan offered a business card that Chris hadn't seen him pull from anywhere. "I want you to have my direct line. If you have any other problems while you're here, call me first. I'm available twenty-four hours a day."

"First as in before calling the police?" Chris asked, trying to better understand what exactly was being offered by this man.

"Did I say that?" Donagan replied, cracking another smile. "I would never suggest that you intentionally circumvent the local authorities. That would be some kind of violation; though I'm not sure exactly what kind, specifically.

"No. I'm just saying that if anything else happens to you while you're *in country*, make me your first call."

"Okay, thanks." Chris still did not understand what conversation he was having or how it came to happen here at the airport where very few people would have known to look for him. "How did you find me here?"

Frank Donagan reached out and shook Chris's hand again, this time more firmly and with greater force. "Great to meet you, Dr. Black. Call me." And then he was gone.

14

Chris looked down into the glass-calm sea as he tied up NAMARI's dive boat to the mooring float bobbing at the surface. His fatigued visage stared back at him. It was a grey day. The sea was grey, as was the sky. In fact, as Chris looked toward the horizon it was difficult to identify exactly where the sea stopped and the sky started.

He recalled many a day like this back home in Carmel and felt the briefest stirrings of home sickness. As far back as middle school, he and his friends found no better canvas for their myriad activities than on the glistening sea. If there were waves, they surfed. If it was too flat to surf, they snorkeled. If for some reason they couldn't snorkel, they'd drag out someone's kayak and spend the afternoon pushing each other off the boat as though it were the only lifeboat from a sunken pirate ship.

Regardless of the activity, Chris recalled fondly the feeling of total exhaustion after endless hours in the ocean; their eyes fried from so much sun reflected off the sea, their muscles exhausted. They would stagger back to one of their homes and proceed to eat everything not tied down in the kitchen. In later years, as the boys grew, weekly trips to the grocery store in Monterey had to be augmented or there would be no food left in the house after one of these sessions.

Now his South African team was back in the Ark Rock MPA, tying up in the vicinity of the wreck that he and Mbeke had found the week before. While NAMARI researchers focused primarily on natural resources such as fishes and invertebrates, shipwrecks were also of interest to them. Over the past decade an increasing interest in "submerged cultural resources" like historically significant wrecks had led the government to add them to NAMARI's list of concerns. The biologists in the group were not happy about it, not unlike the response Chris knew that wrecks had received back in the U.S. There was nothing wrong with a shipwreck. Indeed, back in the U.S. several national marine sanctuaries were established to protect sunken ships. But Chris knew few scientists who wanted to allocate any effort to wrecks when there was never enough money to appropriately survey living creatures of the deep.

All that aside, however, Chris loved diving on wrecks; particularly wrecks that had not yet been properly identified. He understood how the thrill of exploring wrecks could consume a person's life. There was the wreck of a German U-Boat lying on the seafloor at a depth of two-hundred and thirty feet off the coast of New Jersey. At that depth, any dive to the wreck was incredibly dangerous, and it had claimed many lives. Yet many more had searched the wreck in a quest for fame. Or there was the wreck of the Spanish vessel *Atocha* off Florida, a discovery that had continued to yield valuable riches more than two decades after it had first been located.

Chris knew none of the people involved in the discovery of those wrecks, but back in graduate school he had played a small part in the discovery of a sunken coal transport off Massachusetts. A small hunk of coal sat in a place of honor in his office back in California.

After the events of the previous week, the research vessel and all the team's SCUBA equipment had been under guard 24/7 courtesy of

Kathryn. Yet neither Chris nor Kara was willing to let that suffice. They spent a good hour checking all gear closely before ultimately deciding they were ready to get in the water.

Daniel was out for the day at a meeting, so Mbeke was running the boat and would stay at the surface to keep an eye on everything while Chris and Kara were diving. Chris noted that Mbeke was not exactly rushing to get back in the water. After the trauma of the tank valve failure and the shark attack, he couldn't blame him. Daniel's absence was a good thing, Chris thought, because it would give Mbeke a chance to stay connected to the operations without having to get back in the water until he was ready.

The plan for the dive was a simple one. Descend down the mooring line to the seafloor, head due east on a compass heading of ninety degrees until the wreck is encountered, then spend as much bottom time as the depth allowed working to identify the vessel. This was the only dive planned for the day.

Fully equipped in their gear, including cameras for taking images of the wreck, Chris and Kara walked carefully to the stern of the boat. Chris moved out onto the dive step projecting from the stern and to the left of the dive ladder. Kara moved to the right. After receiving the okay from Mbeke, they each did a giant stride off the step into the water.

The giant stride, Chris reflected, was simply and aptly termed. You just added some air to your buoyancy compensator and placed the regulator in your mouth. Then, with one hand pressed against the regulator and the facemask simultaneously to keep them in place when you enter the water, you took a single large step out and away from the boat.

Standing on the dive step looking down at the ladder that had saved his life the previous week, Chris briefly entertained thoughts of sharks. But at this point in his career, if he didn't see one circling the boat or coming toward the surface to consume him, he wasn't going to stay out of the water based on the relatively small threat of a potential attack. Plus, the shark from last week was no doubt long gone by now, and as he'd read online more than once, one still had a higher probability of being killed by a cow or a vending machine.

Once in the water, Kara lead the way to the bow and then down the mooring line to the seafloor. The team was using an oxygen enriched air mixture known as NITROX. NITROX simply augmented the normal twenty-one percent oxygen in the atmosphere by another ten to fifteen percent. The additional oxygen meant less nitrogen entered a diver's bloodstream, which in turn meant that a diver could stay at depth longer and he or she would be less fatigued after completing the dive.

At the bottom, Chris's wrist computer, which had been programmed to the appropriate NITROX mixture, reported an allowable bottom time of thirty minutes. That was not a huge amount of time to find, investigate, and return safely from the wreck, but they would do the best they could.

Kara found the heading on her compass and motioned for Chris to follow her. Visibility underwater had deteriorated since their previous dive to the site. Chris estimated it to be three to four feet. He had to keep a very close eye on Kara's orange fins as he swam behind her; looking away even for a second might result in a dangerous loss of contact.

Meandering through the deeply green water, the only sound Chris heard was his own breathing, amplified by his regulator. Where possible, he watched the seafloor moving past below him in hopes that he would recognize something from his last dive with Mbeke. Glancing at his own compass periodically, he realized that the slight cross-current they were battling at depth was pushing them off course. He and Mbeke had reached the wreck in only five minutes from the mooring line previously. Looking at his watch he realized now that he'd been following Kara more than twice that time.

Tugging on Kara's fin to get her attention, Chris twirled his index finger indicating that he wanted to turn around. Receiving an okay sign from Kara, he then motioned with his hand indicating that he wanted to take a return course that was slightly up current.

Taking the lead on the return, Chris worked his way back west-northwest. He was about to cede defeat for the dive when the side of a wooden vessel emerged from the gloom.

15

Swimming along the edge of the degraded wooden hull, Chris noted that the wreck looked different from what he remembered based on this new angle from which they'd approached. The wreck was most likely a fishing vessel of some kind. The frame was stocky and utilitarian. There appeared to be the remnants of a large hydraulic winch sunken into the deck amidships, which had probably been used to deploy and recover fishing gear back in its day. Much of the wood planking had not done well with the passage of time. As he'd noticed when he'd first encountered the wreck with Mbeke, Chris saw that most exposed surfaces on the wreck were covered with invertebrate life, including huge anemones and vibrantly colored sponges.

The majority of the stern, which was sticking out of the seafloor at a forty-five-degree angle, had collapsed in on itself and there was no discernable evidence of a name to help them identify the wreck. A small debris field extended out from around the wreck onto the open sand. Armed with high-powered, water-proof flashlights, both divers spent several minutes inspecting the scattered pieces of the sunken vessel.

Kara swam over to Chris and motioned to her white PVC dive slate where she'd written the question, "Why is the stern sticking out?" Dive slates had become vital pieces of equipment for scientists, good for collecting data and for communicating with your buddy beyond simple hand signals.

It took Chris a couple of seconds to read what Kara had written; cold water and thick neoprene gloves did not encourage great penmanship. He shrugged his shoulders—the international sign for "I don't know." It was indeed odd to have a wreck sitting on a flat, sandy seafloor protruding so prominently off the bottom. In Chris's experience, most wrecks found their ultimate resting place having settled into the sand more or less uniformly from bow to stern. But for some reason, the stern of this vessel was still sticking out of the sediment.

Kara pointed to her wrist computer and then flashed Chris a single finger followed by four fingers indicating that she had fourteen-hundred PSI remaining in her tank. She motioned toward the bow with one hand and wiggled two extended fingers on the other to simulate a kicking motion. Chris flashed the okay sign and they set off, swimming up over the stern and along what remained of the back deck toward the wheelhouse.

The two-story wheelhouse was still largely intact, though the glass windows that surrounded it had long since perished. Like many of the wrecks Chris had encountered up close, there was a surreal quality to the scene; they were in the presence of a man-made object that was never intended to be submerged. The pair entered the superstructure through a door on the starboard side of upper deck to find the wheel itself was still discernible through the abundant invertebrate life. The bubbles they extruded from their regulators as they exhaled scattered around the roof of the cabin.

Chris surveyed the rest of the space but could find nothing to help him with the vessel's identification. There was a fire extinguisher, now covered in growth, but nothing else was obviously identifiable. At the port side of the wheelhouse there was a narrow spiral staircase leading below decks. Even if it had not been blocked with debris, Chris was doubtful he would have fit through it easily with his SCUBA gear on.

Kara, seeming to read Chris's mind, motioned out the door and downward. Chris nodded and followed her out.

The door to the deck below was still in place. Pulling hard on the door knob, Chris was unable to budge the door. He extracted a flat-ended knife from a sheath on his right calf and stuck it between the door and the door jamb, hoping to pry it open. Kara swam over with her knife and did the same. But all they succeeded in doing was tearing away some of the old, waterlogged wood.

Poking his head in a side window, Chris could see what must have been the galley. There was a dining table immediately in front of him and remnants of a small refrigerator and stove on the other side of the cabin. Both were degraded significantly, but they looked to Chris like appliances from the 1970's. It was not difficult to imagine fishermen sitting there in the galley eating a hearty dinner after a long day of fishing. To his left he could see that the base of the spiral staircase continued to the hold below, but it was blocked by debris.

With both allowable bottom time and air beginning to run low, Chris wanted to take one last look around the bow before they returned to the surface. He signaled to Kara that he wanted to spend five more minutes circling the wreck, then surface directly above the wreck rather than swim back to the mooring line. That would give them a little more time on site.

Much of the bow was embedded deep in the seafloor. Using his flashlight, Chris spotted a hole in the hull several feet in front of him. Approaching the hole, it briefly occurred to Chris that if this were a scene in one of the thrillers his friend Mac made him watch frequently, this is when he'd find a dead body floating ominously on the other side. Flashing his light through the hole he found no bodies, but multiple blue barrels sitting inside the hold tight against one another. The lid of at least one of the barrels was off, but growth and debris prevented him from a clear view of what was inside.

He pulled on the wood around the hole, hoping that it would give way and allow him to look more closely at the contents of the barrels. His mind briefly flashed on his recent experience back in California, where the barrels he and his team had found on the seafloor had contained toxic waste. But the wood did not give way and his mind quickly came back to the job at hand.

Glancing at his dive computer, it was clear to Chris that they would not be able to identify the wreck on this dive. Time was running out. He motioned to Kara that they should begin their ascent to the surface. Before following her, Chris spotted a circular object sitting on the sand to his right. The palm-sized item was heavy in his hand and covered with corrosion and growth. Thinking he'd have some time to look at it on the way back to the dock, he stuck it in one of his buoyancy jacket's pockets and swam after Kara.

16

Jacob Slovo stared out into the black night beyond the wheelhouse window as he drank his coffee from a battered old thermos. The boat rocked gently in the swell as it sat tied up to one of the mooring floats that the government had placed out there. He noted the large dent in the base of the thermos where he'd used it to beat a man's head in the previous week. That man had failed to pay Slovo what he was owed. With this gold recovery taking longer than he expected, Slovo was starting to get anxious about cash flow. They had not even found any gold yet and Slovo was beginning to lose faith.

The boat had no lights on. Slovo did not want to broadcast their presence to any onlookers, even though it was unlikely that anyone would see them out there in the middle of the night. Particularly on a night like tonight. No moon at all. Few stars. Pitch black with the exception of scattered lights along the west side of False Bay, and the larger glow of Cape Town just over the horizon to the north.

Slovo had been awakened from an afternoon nap by an angry call from Willem Greyling complaining that the NAMARI team had been seen out diving on the site in the morning. Greyling wanted gold in his hands, and he wanted the wreck wired to explode if the wrong people tried to get to that gold.

It had taken Slovo several hours to get a plan together, so they had not arrived out on the site until almost 11:00 p.m. Pieter Jonker had spent the first dive of the night looking over the wreck for evidence of the gold. Since Slovo didn't go in the water, they'd hired a diver Jonker knew from the harbor to serve as a buddy. Jonker had said the guy could be trusted, and Slovo reluctantly agreed. Not that he'd had a choice.

During the surface interval after the first dive, Jonker had explained that they could find no evidence of gold around the wreck. "What do you mean you found no gold?" Slovo had asked in frustration. "Nothing?"

"We swam the entire wreck. Twice. It's dark as shit down there, man. You can't see anything," Jonker's buddy had said with some attitude. Slovo had briefly considered cutting off the man's head right there on the spot.

Jonker had jumped in at that point, probably because he could sense that Slovo was considering unsavory actions. "But we couldn't get into the hold. And that is where Greyling said all the gold is. It must still be down there."

"Why couldn't you get into the hold? It's an old wooden wreck," Slovo demanded. "Just rip the planks off! Do I have to do everything here?"

"Part of the wheelhouse—", the buddy had tried to interject, but Slovo had placed his palm on the handle of his machete and said, "Not another word."

"Part of the wheelhouse collapsed and blocked the entrance to the hold," Jonker completed. "But the rest of the hold is solid. I mean, it's um, it's not broken up. We couldn't find another way in without using tools."

"So if the hold hasn't been opened, then the government must not have any of the gold, either," Slovo wondered aloud.

Jonker added, "It doesn't look like anyone has been on that wreck in a long time."

"Then what the hell are they doing out here?" Slovo asked without expecting an answer from Jonker or his buddy.

They'd decided to rig the wreck as Greyling had asked until they could come back with tools to break through the wooden planks surrounding the hold. Jonker's friend, it turned out, was not completely useless after all. He'd brought dynamite and waterproof fuses that he'd stolen from a co-worker in the harbor.

Slovo stepped onto the back deck and stared out into the dark, gripping the rail so hard his knuckles whitened. He didn't think that rigging the wreck to explode made much sense. Blowing it up certainly wouldn't make the gold any easier to recover, just the opposite. He imagined a huge debris field with the gold buried in the sandy seafloor. And if they blew up some government people? That would just invite more government involvement, not less.

Greyling is an idiot, a senile old man, Slovo thought. He hated working for such a man. He never would have if his wife and daughter were still alive. Brief flashes of immense sadness overwhelmed him as an image of his daughter running on the grass in her little flower print dress filled his mind: his girl dashing to her mom, grabbing a hug, then turning around and bouncing back to her daddy. The memory of that gleam in her eyes now nearly incapacitated Slovo. She had been the best thing in his fucked-up world.

And then she had been killed, along with her mom, by someone trying to teach Slovo a lesson; someone who never would have come in contact with his little girl if it weren't for him. He'd learned the lesson, alright. He'd come out the back door of the little house they'd lived in to find his family murdered.

As the murderer stood there smirking, Slovo had slowly taken the machete out of the back of the man's truck and used it to dismember the guy limb by limb.

Slovo's hands shook from a simultaneous rush of sadness, remorse, and then anger. These painful memories always ended with anger. It was what kept him going these days.

The sound of bubbles breaking the surface drew Slovo's attention to the water, where he could see Jonker's dive light slowly making its way toward the surface. He moved to the back of the boat to meet the divers there.

Jonker broke the surface first. "It's done."

17

Having already disposed of one source within NAMARI, Willem Greyling called his conscription to find out what was going on in greater detail. It was a dangerous call, because he didn't want anyone to stumble upon the connection, so he used the disposable cell phone he'd provided the previous month.

"You indicated earlier today that your divers were on the wreck today. What did they find?"

"I don't think they found anything," the source replied. "I was not on the boat today, but in the afternoon staff meeting nothing was mentioned other than the fact that they dove on the wreck instead of collecting data."

"Who were the divers?" Greyling asked.

"Why do you need their names?"

"You would be wise not to fuck with me. Answer my questions."

"Kara McDonnell, Mbeke Tonobu, and a scientist visiting from the U.S."

"The scientist's *name*?"

"Chris Black."

"What does this Black want with the wreck? Why is he diving with NAMARI?"

"As I told you before, Black is a scientist here to help with studying the marine life in the protected area where the wreck happened to sink. Nothing more."

Greyling processed this information. "And yet he was diving on the wreck today and not conducting science. Do you not think that strange?"

"How do you know that?" asked the source.

"I can assure you that you are far from my only source of information. I've been waiting thirty years for this return on my investment. Every detail is important."

"I don't know what to tell you."

"Well, then *I'll* tell *you*. I have evidence that this Black was involved with law enforcement back in the States very recently. He helped to disrupt the dumping of toxic waste in California. My sources tell me that he put people in the hospital and yet was not arrested himself. There are even rumors of some kind of paramilitary unit involved in the event who were working with Black.

"I find it very hard to believe that such a man is here in South Africa, diving on *my* wreck, because of a coincidence!" Greyling added, his voice rising.

The source said nothing.

"I want the addresses for all three of these people."

"I agreed to provide you with information on what is going on at NAMARI, but not with personal addresses."

"You 'agreed' to do whatever I fucking want you to do and not to ask stupid questions or to ignore my requests! " Greyling screamed into the phone. He coughed for more than a minute before adding, "I think you've met several of my associates already. Unless you want to meet them again, I recommend you do what I ask."

18

The day after diving on the wreck, Chris was scheduled to participate in a brief research cruise with a faculty member from the University of Cape Town. The vessel was scheduled to depart from the port in Cape Town at one o'clock, which gave him some time to kill in the morning.

The granny flat that NAMARI had rented for Chris was in the small coastal community of Kommetjie, about ten miles southeast of Cape Town on the western shore of the Cape Peninsula. The larger house next door was currently unoccupied. The neighborhood was primarily made up of single-story, ranch-like houses all within two blocks of a long strip of white sand, appropriately named 'Long Beach.' Every house was walled off and sported a gate, despite being within a gated community.

Chris noted with some dismay that while democracy had come to South Africa, it had not come without significant challenges. Like many of the large urban environments back in the United States, Cape Town's wealth was concentrated among a few, leaving the rest to struggle for survival however they could. Given the deep legacy of racism left by Apartheid, little of the wealth had found its way to the black majority in the country. Walking back and forth to the beach over the past two weeks in Kommetjie, Chris had not seen a single person of color.

After rising at 5:30 a.m., Chris spent the first two hours of the morning relaxing on the outside patio, catching up on email and reading several newspapers online.

Peter Lloyd reported via email that the university's research vessel, the RV *MacGreggor*, was going to be headed to the Galapagos in a little over a month. The trip would include fifteen to twenty students as well as a few faculty and staff. Reading between the lines of Peter's email, it seemed that Abby, Chris's one-time companion, was going on the trip along with another faculty member. Chris suspected that this faculty member was the man Abby was now seeing.

Thinking back to his own first trip to the Galapagos, Chris recalled the utter amazement he had experienced from the moment he got off the plane. He remembered seeing marine iguanas resting on the rocks in front of his hotel within the first fifteen minutes of his arrival. The next morning he'd gone diving with colleagues from the local research station in a place called Tijaretas, which was a protected natural embayment to the north along the coast.

Apart from the extraordinary natural beauty, the bay was distinguished by the fact that it was the location of Charles Darwin's first landfall in the Galapagos. Charles Darwin. That was a great way to begin the trip, Chris recalled.

Well, it was a trip Chris would miss this time around. He smiled at the realization that he would also therefore miss an opportunity for what his friend Mac called "extreme personality expansion," which is no doubt what going on a research cruise with Abby and her new boyfriend would be. Either way, Chris reflected, the decision was already made for him because he was half a world away and planning to stay that way for another six months.

Chris also noted with interest two stories from the *Monterey Herald* back home, one dealt with the clean-up of toxic waste in the Carmel submarine canyon and the other dealt with the ongoing legal prosecution of the consortium responsible for the dumping of that waste.

The CMEx team had ultimately been responsible for bringing the dumpers to justice. For the main three bad guys, that justice had been metaphorical insofar as they were all now dead. For others, such as the members of the larger criminal consortium, it looked from the article as though prosecution was going to take years to complete.

Chris was not surprised that the visceral pain he felt over the incident persisted even six months later. He still felt the absence of his departed colleague every single day. He reached into his right front pocket and extracted a small Swiss Army knife. The colleague's parents had given it to Chris after the funeral. He'd nearly lost it at airport security on the flight to South Africa. Fidgeting with the knife, he used this thumb to pull out the blade briefly before closing it back up.

Knowing that these thoughts could easily consume the rest of his morning, Chris forced himself to get up out of his chair, put away his smartphone, and take off to the beach to catch a few waves before he headed to the port to get on the research vessel. However, when he stepped outside his gate, he found Claudia Schwarz leaning on a white NAMARI land rover.

"Claudia?" Chris hadn't seen her since his brief introduction in Kathryn's office. He didn't think he'd made much of an impression during that meeting. But perhaps he had.

"Hi. Sorry for the surprise drop-by." Claudia was wearing a grey NAMARI hoodie, black sweat pants, and neon orange running shoes. Clearly feeling the need to explain herself, Claudia added, "I heard that you had quite an experience since I saw you last. Added to the earlier shark incident, this suggests you haven't really had the best introduction to Cape Town."

"That isn't how it feels, but to hear you say it out loud, I'll admit that these adventures do sound a bit, um, sub-optimal."

"Sub-optimal? Okay. Anyway, I know you're leaving for a cruise this afternoon, but I thought if you had any time this morning I might show you something."

"Does it involve sharks or hand-to-hand combat?" Chris became more and more intrigued.

"I can guarantee no sharks, and I think combat is probably avoidable." Claudia flashed a smile that Chris found engaging.

"Well then, I'm in! What's the recommended garb for this activity?"

"What you're wearing is fine, but I'd put on some closed-toe shoes."

Chris looked down at his flip flops. "So you're saying there may be some kicking after all, eh? Be right back."

To Chris's surprise, Claudia drove as fast as he did. And she talked nearly as quickly as she drove. During the brief forty-minute drive, Chris learned that Claudia had gone to university in London before returning to South Africa to work at NAMARI and to live with her brother.

Claudia asked a lot of questions. But she had a habit of answering the questions herself, often with new questions. Before he had a chance to say much of anything, he was standing at the southernmost point on the Cape of Good Hope, a rocky promontory jutting out from the South African mainland. The grasslands they'd driven through as they approached the Cape Point National Park reminded Chris of the Sonoma coastline back in California. The grasses were punctuated here and there with rocky outcroppings and low-lying bushes. An important difference he'd noted quickly, however, was that unlike in California, these grasslands featured free-ranging zebra and not a small number of baboons.

The abundant wildlife in the road forced Claudia to slow to a mere mortal's speed, which had given Chris a chance to appreciate it all up close. Though the encounter with the white shark had been impactful, Chris realized that it wasn't until that moment, in the presence of zebra, that he truly realized he was in Africa. Watching six of them trot by within feet of the vehicle was, to Chris, a realization of a lifelong goal; he'd always wanted to come to this continent.

Now, leaning on the substantial guardrail and looking south from his perch some two hundred feet above the sea's surface, Chris found himself in the unique position of having the Atlantic Ocean to his right and the Indian Ocean to his left. He reflected on the fact that Antarctica was somewhere over the horizon to the south and that he was at that moment closer to it than he'd ever been before. Though Chris didn't think in terms of bucket lists, he knew that if he were to have such a list, Antarctica would be at or near the top.

"What do you think?" Claudia asked from Chris's left.

"It doesn't suck." Chris watched the waves crash upon the rocks below.

"It doesn't suck? I've never been to California, but that sounds like something I imagine a Californian might say. Kinda cool sounding, maybe a little bit aloof."

"Thank you for sharing this extraordinary natural treasure with me." Chris hoped he sounded both honest and a bit sarcastic.

They stood quietly for several minutes as Chris absorbed his surroundings.

"Can I ask you a question?"

Another one? Chris thought, but aloud he said, "Sure. But be aware that I might answer aloofly."

"What is it like to fight for your life? I mean, how do you even know that you can do that? Are all Americans trained to defend themselves at any moment?"

Chris sighed internally at the questions. He knew that they were legitimate, but he was tired of talking about it, particularly with people who didn't understand. But then again, Claudia was one of the most direct individuals he'd ever met. He turned around slowly and made eye contact with her.

"It's terrible. Horrifying. It basically sucks. But I have to admit that there's some measure of exhilaration, too."

"Exhilaration?"

"I don't know why I'm admitting this to you . . ."

"Probably because you sense I'm truly insightful, and you're looking for insight."

"Perhaps, perhaps," Chris shook his head slightly at her forwardness.

"Are you an adrenaline junkie like I understand most Californians are?"

"Do I need to be here for this conversation?" Chris let some frustration creep into his voice. "Are you going to give me a chance to answer? Or is your mind made up? About Californians in general and me in particular?"

"I'm sorry. Yes, please, do continue. I get too excited sometimes."

Chris regretted his frustration. "Look, I don't have all the answers. Maybe I have no answers at all. And you can probably tell that I don't have all the distance I need, either."

Pulling down the neck of his T-shirt until the bandage on his chest was exposed, Chris added, "I've literally still got open wounds from my most recent experience."

Chris let his stare wonder back up the path they'd hiked down to get to this point. There were only two other people visible anywhere in the area.

A few more seconds passed and then he said, "I guess I don't know how to answer your original question. Or at least I don't know how to answer it anymore. You aren't the first person to ask. I guess I'm burned out."

Claudia looked down at her feet for a few seconds then said, "I was fourteen when I went with my family on a trip to Johannesburg to visit relatives. It was the type of trip no fourteen-year-old wants to take. But my brother, Charlie, who was eight at the time, was very excited, so I did my best as a big sister to be enthusiastic.

"We'd only been there for two days when we were driving back to the hotel from my great aunt's house. I remember not feeling well from all the cheese and butter we'd had to eat. I remember what the rental car smelled like. I can remember the pattern on the back of the front seat—because I'd stared at it for such a long time—and what the door handles looked like.

"And I remember how utterly terrified and helpless I felt when, while stopped at a traffic light, two masked thugs shattered the driver's side window and shot both my parents."

Chris closed his eyes and dropped his chin to his chest, "I'm so sorry . . ."

"They didn't even try to take the car," Claudia continued." They just grabbed my mom's purse from the front seat and took off. They killed my parents over a purse!"

She reached up under the glasses to rub tears out of her eyes.

"I felt so helpless. So completely fucking worthless," Claudia's voice cracked. "Of course the guys were never caught, at least not for killing my parents. For all I know they went on to terrorize many more people. Maybe they're still doing it now!"

"Claudia, I'm sorry I sounded flippant or frustrated. You obviously understand what I'm talking about."

Claudia kept talking as though Chris weren't there. Looking down from their perch, her arms sweeping outward, she added, "So when I heard that you defended your family at the botanical gardens, and that you'd done so back in California as well, I was just so mystified that I had to seek you out. I had to find out how someone can act with such certainty at such horrifying moments."

Chris struggled for the words to respond. "Fourteen is very young, Claudia. I never had to face real danger until I was well into my twenties. I'm sure I would have been just as scared as you were and certainly no more responsive."

Chris paused for a minute and then continued, "I'm so sorry that you had to experience that. How did your brother handle it?"

"He was traumatized for years. It didn't help that we weren't that close back then. *And* I was a teenager. But when it finally dawned on me that he was the only real family I had left, I made a better effort."

"What is he up to these days?" Chris asked, trying to focus on the positive.

Claudia briefly tensed before answering, "Charlie's now a student at UCT. He's in the biology program and really loves it."

"That's excellent, you must be proud of him."

"You have no idea. So that's all you have for me? There's no special training or secret military experience?"

"Oh, there was training. Mostly getting beat on by my friends. I think that helped more than anything."

"You must have tough friends," Claudia observed.

"Yeah, they are pretty tough. One's a former Navy SEAL. Now *his* friends are a truly intimidating group. They've helped me out on more than one occasion."

Continuing to look back up the path periodically as he spoke, Chris noted that two men positioned well up the path seemed to be staring at him and Claudia. One of them was a tall black man, the other a shorter white guy. They were too far away for him to see anything else. He wondered to himself whether it was something needed to be concerned about.

Claudia followed his stare and asked, "What do you see up there?"

"Probably nothing. Just jumpy, I guess. Not everyone can be after me all the time, right?"

"Those two men? You think they're looking at us?"

The two guys had moved out of sight. "They were looking at us, alright. But it was probably nothing."

"Maybe they think you have me down here to propose or something and they're jealous."

Chris couldn't help but burst out laughing.

19

Two hours later Chris walked up the gangway onto the research vessel *Polar Sea,* South Africa's newest addition to the fleet. The midday sun, reflected off the spotless white paint of the new ship, was blinding. The ship was three hundred feet long, with a crew of twenty and a scientific complement ranging from five to twenty depending on the project, all spread across six decks. A helicopter sat on a pad near the stern, and two single-person submersibles were visible on the aft deck.

The pre-cruise rush to get the ship ready for departure was in full force, every corridor bustling with activity. Lugging a duffel bag over one shoulder and a computer case over the other, Chris dodged other equivalently burdened people, ducked under low overhead hatchways, and eventually made his way to the main scientific lab.

There he found Dr. Ling Lee, the principal investigator on the project and a dear friend of Chris's from graduate school. Known to most by her nickname, Karen, she had been on the fast track since grad school and was now one of the leading experts on deep water corals in the world.

Unlike the more well-known reef-building corals of the tropics, deep water corals did not form reefs but instead grew into elaborate, multi-colored, plant-like structures reaching heights of five feet or more.

If left undisturbed, some corals were estimated to live longer than one thousand years.

Karen was standing with her back to Chris, directing a man and woman who were likely graduate students. At five foot ten inches she was taller than both her students, with long black hair that was slowly accumulating a few gray highlights. She had worked at Yale, in Paris, and was now at the University of Cape Town.

"I'm surprised the United Nations let you go long enough to participate in this cruise."

Karen had worked with the UN on a couple of different occasions, and Chris never let her forget it. "I don't know how they'll get along without you."

Turning quickly, Karen looked at Chris, then at her two students and replied, "Ladies and gentlemen, I give you Dr. Chris Black, scourge of toxic waste dumpers the world over!"

While receiving an energetic hug from his good friend, Chris noted with surprise that Claudia was seated at a computer workstation in the back of the lab. He knew someone from NAMARI would be on the cruise, but she had somehow neglected to tell him that morning that it was going to be her. She conspicuously did not turn around when Karen announced Chris's arrival to the group.

"It has been too long," Karen continued with enthusiasm. Then, in a more subdued tone, she added, "I am so sorry about what happened in Carmel Bay and all the trouble that you went through. I wish I could have been back in California to support you."

"We definitely could have used you out there."

"Right! I'm not sure what I could have offered a couple of tough guys like you and Mac," she said, looking Chris over.

"And Hendrix. Do you remember him from that trip we took to Israel? I would have been toast without him."

"How could I forget? I've never seen anyone watch a room the way he did. He kept buying me beers at that sketchy bar in Tel Aviv all the while sizing up each person who entered the bar for the potential threats they represented. I've never seen anything like it."

After reminiscing for another ten minutes, and introducing Chris to her graduate students, Karen suggested, "Get your stuff up to your stateroom, which is one deck up. We should be underway within thirty minutes, then we'll convene in the galley at 4:00 p.m. for the pre-cruise briefing. Don't be late. You are now central to this mission."

"Uh, oh. What do you mean? I thought I was just an observer on this cruise. You know, 'arm candy.'"

"Oh you're definitely arm candy, don't worry about that. But my backup pilot is down with a migraine, so I'm going to need you to drive the other sub. You're the only other scientist on board—in fact, you're probably the only other scientist in all of Africa—who is trained on these particular subs right now."

Chris's eyes widened at the revelation that the next two days were not going to be the simple diversion he'd expected them to be. He grabbed a bound copy of the sub operations manual from a shelf to his right. "I guess I have some reviewing to do," he said as he headed out the hatch. Looking toward Claudia briefly, he noticed that she had yet to turn around. Thinking back to their conversation in the morning, Chris expected that she'd be back with more questions sooner rather than later.

After stowing his gear and looking through the manual, Chris came back out into the brilliant sunshine to watch as the ship left port. This had been his custom as long as he could remember. Leaving port had always represented to him a ceremonial departure from the comfortable confines of civilized society and an entry into the great unknown.

Leaning against a rail on his elbows, Chris looked aft to the two subs sitting on the deck and beyond to the churning waters generated by the ship's massive propellers. Cape Town's Table Mountain loomed above their vessel, slowly receding as they gained speed. He could hear and see much of the crew out in the fresh air, all taking in the same spectacle as they motored out to sea.

And then, without warning, Claudia joined him. She leaned on the rail next to him, her left arm in direct contact with his own, and her eyes gleaming as she looked at him.

"Funny meeting you here," she offered

Funny indeed, Chris thought as he struggled to come up with something witty to say.

Nothing came. He was drawn back, instead, to a book he'd read in college by Thomas Mann, called *A Death in Venice*. There was a particular passage about "the solitary" that had fascinated Chris during his undergraduate days.

As he'd attempted to explain to his friend Mac on more than one occasion—under a barrage of sarcastic barbs—to "the solitary" person, interpersonal communications are quite a bit more complicated than they are for more gregarious people.

"You, Mac, talk to a woman and you hear the words coming out of her mouth," Chris had explained.

"Uh, right," Mac answered, pretending to step back from the crazy person in front of him. "Don't you?"

"Yes of course, you idiot," Chris replied, exasperated. "But were she to reach out and touch my shoulder casually, as normal people do, I would become fixated on that personal contact. I would read more into it than likely was intended. You see?"

During the most recent iteration of this conversation Mac had then reached out and put his hand on Chris's shoulder. "Don't worry, I won't tell anyone."

"Tell anyone what?" Chris replied.

"That the chief scientist on this cruise has literally gone off the deep end," Mac said. As he got up and left the lab he'd added, "And don't read too much into that hand I just placed on your shoulder."

"What are you smiling about?" Claudia asked, drawing Chris back to the present.

"Thomas Mann and Robert Johnson," Chris said.

"I've heard of Thomas Mann, but not of Robert Johnson. Should I have?"

"He's really an acquired taste. I'll introduce you to him some time. So what are you doing out here?"

"NAMARI generally sends someone out on any research cruise that uses a government vessel."

"And you drew the short straw on this one?" Chris asked, wondering how long he could continue with his arm in contact with hers.

"Actually, I volunteered."

"Volunteered?"

"Quite. You see I wanted to spend some time watching the famous Dr. Chris Black at work."

"And this morning?"

"Oh, that was just added fun."

Just then Karen Lee emerged from the hatch behind them and beckoned Chris back into the lab. "The weather window for tomorrow afternoon is not looking great. We need to get ready to dive at first light."

"We can talk more later." Claudia squeezed Chris's arm before she walked away.

By 0500 the next morning, the *Polar Sea* had reached the dive site and was holding station over the precise location where the submersibles would be deployed. Having spent much of the evening reviewing submersible protocols and discussing the data collection plan, Chris and Karen were ready.

The *DeepSea 3000* was a single-person submersible capable of operating down to three thousand feet water depth. Unlike other submersibles used for scientific research around the world, with the *DeepSea 3000* the scientist was the pilot. The scientist/pilot sat upright in a seat with the approximate dimensions of a coach-class airline seat. The sub was controlled by pedals under each foot—up/down, left/right, forward/reverse—and by three small touch screens mounted on the hull about chest height for the seated pilot. The screens controlled cameras, lights, and the manipulator arm and they tracked the balance of oxygen and carbon dioxide inside the sub. An armored Plexiglas dome was set above the pilot's head so that he/she could see clearly in all directions.

Chris had been trained on the *DeepSea 3000* years ago on a project in New England near the end of grad school. As he sat reclined on his bunk reading through the manual and waiting for word over the intercom that operations were a go, he recalled how exciting it had been to pilot the sub for the first time. Though he'd experienced a great deal over the years, sitting on the seafloor alone at twelve hundred feet down had been an experience he'd never forget.

The intercom buzzed. "Chris, this is Karen. We are *go* for diving. Please proceed to the back deck to complete the pre-dive checklist."

Chris reached over his head to cue his mike. "Copy that. I'm on my way."

He was dressed only in red fleece long underwear and wool socks. At the depths they would be working today, the water was very cold, and that cold would be effectively transferred through the sub's hull. But on the other hand, he would be in a very small space exhaling regularly, which would warm the space considerably. So he had to be prepared for both shivering and sweating. The red fleece was the same outfit he'd worn back during that first mission, so Chris was counting on the fact that it would work again. The fact that he was running around the ship in his underwear didn't seem to bother anyone.

The pre-dive checklist took fifteen minutes. Claudia assisted Chris, while one of Karen's graduate students assisted her. The goal of the checklist was to make sure all systems were operational before the sub went in the water, and it gave the pilots one last chance to familiarize themselves with the technology that would keep them alive while underwater.

Sitting in one of the subs, hatch open, Chris could feel Karen's eyes on him as he worked with Claudia. He could feel her inquiring mind. Karen had frequently unnerved him in grad school with her penetrating insights about his love life. And he also knew she wouldn't let it go by without comment. Fortunately, that conversation would have to wait.

"You're good to go, Santa," Claudia said.

"Santa? Oh, very funny. Do you write your own material?"

"I don't have to write anything. With outfits like yours the comedy writes itself."

Karen was operating *Sub One* and was the first to be put in the water. Similar to the remotely operated vehicle (ROV) operations that Chris was so familiar with back in California, deployment of the submersible required being picked up off the back deck of the research vessel by a large crane. The crane then swung out over the side of the vessel and lowered the sub into the water.

As the deck manager had pointed out to the scientists on multiple occasions when they'd prepared the night before, "It may seem like a routine ROV deployment from your perspectives, but I can assure you that it's not. Putting a person in the sub changes everything."

One of Karen's students, a woman named Jessica, had asked, "What do you mean?"

"Well, if the crane were to accidentally drop an ROV on deck from ten feet up," Hans, the deck manager, had replied, "or if an ROV broke off its harness and fell over the side during a deployment never to be seen again, all we'd have lost is technology, which is replaceable. But when you have a person involved . . ."

"Oh, I see." The excitement in the room had dimmed noticeably as everyone processed what Hans was trying to say.

While Karen bobbed at the surface, checking her radio communications with mission control back in the ship's science lab, Chris was picked up off the deck by the crane and swung out over the side in *Sub Two*. Each pilot would communicate directly with mission control at twenty-minute intervals to report life support readings and would be in constant communication with the other sub while submerged.

"*Sub One* to *Sub Two*. Chris, how do you read me?" Karen asked.

"Loud and clear *Sub One*. Ready to dive."

"Okay, let's descend as quickly as we can. Keep me in sight during descent, and then we'll separate once we reach the seafloor."

"Copy that," Chris replied. "See you on the bottom."

20

Piloting the sub was easy during the slow descent to the seafloor. The only sound came from the sub's thrusters, which sounded to Chris like an electric golf cart might if operated under water. This gave Chris time to reflect on the briefing Karen had given the science team the night before. She'd explained that the importance of deep-sea corals for the communities that live on the seafloor had been identified only recently. As the use of ROVs and submersibles increased dating back to the late 1980s, scientists began to find corals around the world. They found them on submerged volcanoes, also known as seamounts, and on the steep walls of submarine canyons. They found them in the tropics and at the poles.

Chris knew from his own research that corals were likely distributed much more widely at some point in the distant past, but human activities such as bottom trawling had likely impacted them in areas accessible to fishing. The steep walls of canyons and seamounts were, Chris reflected, the last refuge of these long-lived, but very fragile organisms because it was difficult to drag nets on steep terrain.

Karen had explained that the last visit to this particular location was approximately fifteen years ago. A scientist named Ernst Kestrel had used an ROV to look for deep water fishes and found an extensive garden of corals in the process. Budget cuts to scientific agencies had prevented anyone from re-visiting the site until this cruise.

Fifteen minutes later Karen reported, "Bottom in sight on sonar. According to my computer display, we should be directly in the middle of what Dr. Kestrel referred to as a "coral garden" when he was here fifteen years ago. Stand by for visual."

Chris was positioned approximately fifteen feet above Karen's sub, which was clearly visible in the pitch-black water at six hundred feet water depth because of the bright lights mounted on the sub's bow. He could see the position of the two subs on his own display.

The display depicted a digital map of the study area. The positions of the vessel and the two subs were superimposed over that map. Chris knew from previous experience that the vessel's position was updated constantly in real time by the Global Positioning System, or GPS, network of satellites. The accuracy of the satellite-derived position was on the order of meters to centimeters depending on where you were in the world and how many satellites you we connected with.

But GPS didn't work underwater, so an alternative had to be developed. Chris had noted during the pre-dive check that the subs were equipped with the same acoustic tracking system that his *Seaview* ROV used back in California. Sound travelled so much further underwater than in the air, that it proved an effective way to track equipment underwater. A pinger on the sub was in near constant communication with a hydrophone that was deployed over the side of the research vessel. That communication produced a position of each sub relative to the known position of the ship, thus providing an accurate position on the map for the subs.

Karen's voice came through his headset, "Okay, I see the bottom. I see..."

"Karen, repeat that last. What can you see?" Chris maneuvered his sub to the left of Karen's and halted his descent at ten feet off the seafloor.

A few more seconds passed before Karen said, "Look at the seafloor. It's covered in broken corals. They've all been knocked down."

As Karen's words came through Chris's headset, the carnage on the seafloor below him began to make sense. He was looking at once-tall corals lying broken on the seafloor. Had he not seen some of these corals elsewhere in the world, standing tall and healthy, he might not have understood how troubling it was for Karen to find these thousand-year-old organisms destroyed. But as it was, he could feel Karen's shock coming through the silence.

"Trawling?" Chris asked.

"Very possibly," Karen said. "Many local bottom trawlers were hit hard by the recent financial crises and aren't operating anymore. But this could have happened long before that."

Chris had participated in research on bottom trawling years before off the west coast of the U.S. Bottom trawls were large nets configured to be dragged along the seafloor to catch fish that lived on or very near the bottom. He knew that in some habitats, such as low relief sandy areas, bottom trawls could effectively catch fish without noticeably impacting the seafloor. But in other habitats, such as areas with tall, deep-water corals like these, bottom trawls effectively leveled everything in their paths.

The irony, as Chris had pointed out on more than one occasion to groups of fishermen and managers alike, was that knocking down the corals actually hurt the very fish populations that the trawlers were seeking to catch. Removing the structure removed hiding places for small fish, rendered them vulnerable to predation long before they might fill a net. That meant that the fishing community would have fewer fish to catch in future years.

"Looking at sonar I'm not seeing much to the north, west, or south," Karen said. "But to the east at about six hundred feet the seafloor starts to rise steeply. There might be something there. Let's head that direction."

Chris nodded instinctively, although he knew Karen couldn't see him. "You have the high definition camera on your sub Chris. Please collect some video as we go. We need to document what we're seeing. I'll take still photos from here."

"Copy that. Will do." Chris used the touch screen to his right to cue up the video camera. He engaged the camera mounted on the sub's manipulator arm. This gave him the chance to position the camera out in front of the sub, looking downward at a forty-five-degree angle. A small window in the corner of the touch screen provided the live feed from the video, so Chris could make sure he was getting the video they needed as he piloted the sub to the east.

Ten minutes later, as the two subs began the slow progression up the steep slope, they found abundant corals distributed over a patch of seafloor equal to the size of a football field. Orange, pink and blue corals emerged more than five feet into the water column. Both Chris and Karen had to carefully monitor buoyancy in order to avoid knocking down any of the corals.

"This is amazing," Karen reported over the radio.

"I feel like reciting some Dr. Seuss," Chris replied. "The diversity of colors and shapes is unreal. I've seen corals before, but not like this. I guess we're looking at another example of a natural refugium provided by the steepness of the slope."

"I think you're right," Karen said. "With rare exception, wherever we find steep topography underwater, we find more living structure on the seafloor. This is encouraging compared with what we saw behind us."

Karen spent the next thirty minutes talking to a reporter back on the *Polar Sea* about what she was seeing while Chris recorded video, until the deck operator interrupted to indicate that the weather was picking up and that both subs should surface immediately.

"That sounds like an invitation to pull the lever," Chris suggested.

One of the enduring disappointments from Chris's submersible training was that he never got the opportunity to pull the lever located under the pilot's seat. That lever disconnected the sub's hull from the ballast weights and power supply, sending the positively buoyant hull rocketing toward the surface. The training manual had described it as "the lever of last resort," only to be used in life-threatening situations. No one he knew had ever pulled the lever, but every scientist he'd met that used the subs wanted to.

"The lever? You want to see a life-threatening situation?" Karen asked. "Just pull that lever and you will."

Chris mocked a sigh and responded, "How far we've come from those good old grad school days. You've gone all mainstream on me."

"Mainstream, eh? I'll show you mainstream once we're back on deck. That is, if you aren't too busy cuddling with your new friend Claudia!"

"Um, *Subs One* and *Two*, this is mission control. Please be advised that your communications are now being broadcast shipwide."

21

Much of the extraordinary disappointment experienced by the research team at having found Kestrel's coral garden destroyed had been mediated by the discovery of the healthy corals up on the steeper slopes. After two hours of post-dive checks on the subs, and another two hours post-processing the video imagery that Chris and Karen had collected, the team relaxed in the video lounge to decompress.

Looking around the room at the assembled characters—Karen and her immediate team on the comfortable couch, undergraduates sitting on every other surface, the sub operations crew lingering in the back of the room, closest to the food and drinks—Chris reflected on the fact that he was nearly as far away from Carmel, California, as he could be on planet Earth, but the assembled group could just as easily be his own crew back on the RV *MacGreggor*. It was never clear exactly what made a team cohesive, but somehow the model worked everywhere and over and over again. Science depended on it.

Then another constant in the universe of field science revealed itself when the group began to discuss what movie to watch. Chris had been present for this dynamic more times than he could count, and he took this opportunity to step out of the lounge. He grabbed a thick orange exposure jacket from a hook on the wall in the lab and stepped out into the crisp night air.

Chris could feel the pangs of nostalgia creep in as he thought about his own team. In the months prior to their discovery of the toxic waste in the Carmel submarine canyon, the team had been, as his close friend Mac was fond of saying, "firing on all cylinders." There was no project they couldn't handle.

And then came Gretchen's death. The team had not really been firing on any cylinders since then, Chris knew. And he knew that it was largely his fault. The violence and death had been devastating for the whole team. Mac, for instance, didn't leave the ROV lab for weeks after the incident. And Chris's dog, Thiggo, hadn't been the same, either.

And as he'd wallowed in his sadness, frustration, and guilt, Chris had let the team gradually fall apart. Mac would never be far away, but the students and other staff had slowly taken on work with other projects and were now spread to the four corners of the globe. One of the two students named Diana, Chris had learned recently, had taken a position at the south pole working on climate change in what Chris imagined was the most desolate spot on Earth. Desolate, but incredibly interesting. And his former research technician, Alex, now had a job at a research station in the Galapagos.

And then there was Abby. Chris liked to think that he led an authentic life, that he was honest with himself at all times. That was why he could honestly admit that pushing Abby out of his mind had been the best thing for him under the circumstances. He didn't need to focus on the fact that Abby had apparently established a new relationship with one of the other professors at the CMEx.

"We have to stop meeting like this!" Claudia approached Chris from the right. "People will talk."

"Oh, they're already talking," Chris replied, thinking about Karen's broadcast to the entire ship earlier in the day.

"Let them talk. They need to talk about something, might as well be about us."

Chris smiled at the way Claudia expressed herself so openly. "Fair enough. Did they decide on a movie yet in there?"

"Not that I could tell. Karen was trying to get them to watch something called '*From Dusk to Dawn*,' but not everyone agreed. Do you know it?"

"Oh, yeah. I was with Karen the first time we both saw that movie back in grad school. Not a good film, but we've both used it since to emphasize different points in lectures."

"Like what?"

Chris paused for a second and then explained, "Karen likes to emphasize that it starts out as one type of movie, and then becomes something else altogether by the end. Which I guess is a metaphor for much in life."

Claudia nodded. "That's true. And what about you?"

Chris smiled. "On my end, I'm a big fan of the director's alleged pitch for the film before he made it."

Claudia waited, so Chris continued, "'The bad guys meet the 'badder' guys.' I'm particularly fond of that one. I don't watch it anymore," Chris added. "But that moment when the vampires show up . . . I wouldn't mind being surprised like that more often."

"Really? Maybe this will surprise you." Claudia leaned in to kiss him, leaned back to smile and look at him, and then leaned in to kissed him again. "Surprised?"

"Er, um, why stop there? I don't think I fully understand what you're getting at. I need more information."

Claudia kissed him longer this time. And this time Chris kissed back.

"Whew! That is a huge relief. I've wanted to do that every day since you arrived at NAMARI. I can't get any work done."

"Well, the last thing I want to do is distract anyone from their work. And I'm sure Kathryn would not be happy with me if she knew."

"Oh she knows. I'm sure most of them know, the women at least."

Chuckling again at Claudia's openness, Chris asked, "You don't think Daniel or Mbeke are clued in?"

"I'd say that is very unlikely."

"What's unlikely?" Karen asked as she joined Chris and Claudia at the rail. "That anyone is aware that Claudia's after you?"

"Jesus! Is nothing sacred around here?" Chris asked the dark waters below. "And how does everyone keep sneaking up on me at the rail like this?"

"Indeed. One wonders how you've made it this far," Karen said. "How's your other, Claudia?"

"He's great. Thank you for asking."

"I had him in my invertebrate ecology course last fall. He was a bright student. I think he received a rare 'A.' But I haven't seen him around the department this semester."

Chris noticed a little of the gleam go out of Claudia's eyes for the briefest of moments.

"Well, I mean he's been sick for a while and hasn't been in school. But we're hopeful he will be able to return soon. I know that he would like to work with you for graduate school. That's all he talks about."

"Really? It's Charlie, right? Please tell him he's welcome. I think that our discovery here of this new coral field is going to leave us with a great deal of work to do. I could use his help."

Then, turning to Chris, Karen asked, "So the rest of the week we'll be going far offshore to sample plankton biomass. I know you how much you enjoy that."

"Ha. Your memory serves you well, at least in that regard."

"Not a fan of plankton? Who doesn't like plankton?" Claudia asked.

"Chris Black hates plankton, that's who," Karen answered. "Want to tell her why?"

Chris shook his head slowly. "Poop."

"Poop?" Claudia asked.

"Yes, poop," Karen answered for Chris. "One of our roommates in grad school studied copepods for his dissertation work. You know, these very small crustaceans? Specifically, Ron studied copepod poop. Interesting, right? Well, our Chris overdid it trying to support said roommate, and ended up participating in one plankton cruise too many. He's never been the same."

"That sounds pretty interesting, but what's the big deal?" Claudia looked from Karen to Chris.

"It's not," Chris said, "but it *is* true. I, excuse me Claudia, hate f-ing copepods. Never again."

"I still don't get it."

Karen explained, "The bottom line is that long days at sea, looking at poop under a microscope, without ever getting in the water, is not Chris's cup of tea."

"No diatom tests for Christmas this year. Got it."

Karen laughed. "That's right. But let's compare notes later, Claudia. I can give you lots of good gift suggestions.

"Seriously though, Chris, do you want to catch the helicopter ride back tomorrow morning? There's room for you and your stuff. Well, I assume your stuff. You didn't bring much stuff did you?"

"Minimal stuff," Chris answered.

"Great. Claudia, you are also scheduled for the flight back. And you'll report to NAMARI on what we found out here?"

"Yes. Kathryn wants to hear from me as soon as I'm back, so probably tomorrow afternoon. Anything in particular you want me to report?"

Karen handed Claudia a small thumb drive. "Images, video clips, and maps are all on here. I'll give them a full report when I return next week, but it would be great if you can give them an overview. Kathryn may want to start requesting ship and sub time to come back out here ASAP. I'll catch you two in the morning before liftoff."

With that, Chris noted, Karen swept out as quickly as she'd swept in. He turned to Claudia, smiled as suavely as he could, and asked, "So, where were we?"

22

Two days later, Chris walked into the lobby of NAMARI's office in downtown Cape Town to meet up with Daniel, report to Kathryn, and, he had to admit, see Claudia.

He'd received an email message from Karen the previous night. She was way offshore, but satellite technology had improved dramatically and email contact was now fairly regular. The goal of Karen's message had been to warn Chris about Claudia. In her mind, Claudia was coming on too strong and that there was something off about that. She encouraged him to be careful.

Chris had learned to trust Karen's instincts, and he agreed that he had thought her advances surprising as well. Not that he had never been courted by a woman, but something seemed off. But he also admitted to himself that he enjoyed talking with her. So for now he was going to go with it and see what happened.

Chris was impressed by the lobby of NAMARI; wall to ceiling glass, a large cetacean skeleton hanging from the ceiling, and multiple kiosks at which visitors could follow NAMARI's various adventures using touch screens.

Heading toward the bank of elevators, Chris spotted another colleague he'd met at a party at Kathryn's house the first week he'd arrived. The man was an archaeologist working for NAMARI and the University of Cape Town. He and Chris had talked for hours about the various things they'd seen underwater. It had been an interesting conversation, Chris thought, because all he talked about was living resources, while all Dr. Brody had talked about was shipwrecks. But since they both used SCUBA and ROVs to conduct their work, there was a great deal to discuss. Kathryn had had to kick them out of the house long after everyone else had departed.

"Dr. Brody, I presume," Chris said as he approached the elevator. "How are you, sir?"

"Ah, Dr. Black! Still chasing all that bioclutter?" One of the enjoyable points of contention in their party conversation had been the notion of what Brody called "bioclutter." It seemed that to archaeologists who study undersea wrecks, the very living material that so fascinated Chris and his scientific colleagues—such as dense clouds of fish swimming along the bottom and tall sponges and corals attached to substrates—presented a huge impediment to their archaeological work. It was difficult to study a seventeenth century wooden ship if it was covered with living organisms, hence the bioclutter.

"You know, I've been thinking about that," Chris replied. "While my biology may clutter your view of a wreck, insofar as humans are biological, wouldn't the wrecks that they spread around my seafloor really be the ultimate clutter?"

"Touché," Dr. Body said. "Did you just get back from that corals cruise with Dr. Lee?"

The elevator door opened and Chris followed Dr. Brody in. "Yes, as a matter of fact, I did. It was pretty fascinating."

"I heard that the onset of Dr. Slaughter's migraine gave you a chance to dive in the sub."

"That's correct. We found a lot of dead corals . . ."

Chris's thought process was interrupted when the door to the elevator opened. A very tall black man and a short Caucasian man with white hair stepped in.

Dr. Brody said, "This elevator is going up, you realize."

The small guy started to answer, but the larger man stopped him. "Yes," he replied, then turned his back to Chris and faced the elevator door.

"So you were saying, Chris? You found dead corals and, what exactly?" As Chris listened to Dr. Brody's question, he could tell that the larger was listening. The smaller guy seemed uninterested, but the bigger guy was definitely listening.

"We, um, sorry. I got distracted for a second. We found a large area of corals that had been knocked down, but then found an even larger area up the slope somewhat in which the corals were flourishing."

"Very interesting. What are you doing next?"

At that moment the elevator stopped at the last floor to which the public was allowed access. The two men stepped off. While the small man kept walking away, the large guy turned and made eye contact with Chris. He held his gaze until the door closed.

23

As soon as the elevator closed, Slovo grabbed his cell phone. They had just been pressuring their contact at NAMARI to provide more information. Greyling had not wanted them to do that, but Slovo was sick of waiting and he thought that their contact was getting too complacent. Jonker, who had missed the significance of the interaction in the elevator, saw that Slovo had stopped. He walked back down the hall to ask what was going on.

"In the elevator, talking with that marine archaeologist," Slovo said, "that was the American, Chris Black."

"*That* was Black? He doesn't seem like a big problem to me," Jonker replied. "I should just go upstairs and take him out right now."

Slovo ignored Jonker's comment. "Black was working with Brody. Brody's the guy that loves to get himself in the papers with colorful pictures of shipwrecks. I wasn't buying all that bullshit about Black not being interested in the wreck before, and now I *know* that it's total bullshit. They are up to something."

"If they are working on the wreck, why haven't they blown up yet? We wired that thing carefully."

"Didn't you hear our contact upstairs tell us that Black had been offshore on a separate project for three or four days? He hasn't had time.

Or maybe they unwired it. I knew I shouldn't have sent you two idiots down there."

"Hey, we wired it well. And you know what? If they do blow it up, the beauty of the explosives we got from my buddy is that the explosion will look like some old military ordinance accidentally blew up. No one is going to know it was intentional. No one."

Slovo admitted to himself that he hadn't considered that possibility. An explosion *would* make recovering the gold much harder. But it would be good if the authorities were confused about who and why the explosion occurred.

He called Greyling.

"I trust you are calling with good news," Greyling answered. "Has the weather cleared enough to return to the wreck?"

"Yes. But we've had some difficulty obtaining some of the tools we need to penetrate the hull."

"That is not good news. I thought I was clear that I didn't want to be bothered until there was something positive to report."

"We just saw the American, Black, in an elevator at the government building with an archaeologist; the one that is on TV all the time."

"And?"

"And we haven't really been following any of them so far, but I would like to start. I want to have Black followed everywhere he goes, see who he talks to. I need your resources to make that happen."

"Fine. Jonker will know who to contact."

"What about tools? What can you do to get us what we need?"

"Contact me in the morning, and I'll give you instructions."

24

Chris Black surfaced from the first dive of the day to find another dive boat tied up alongside NAMARI's vessel. He passed his equipment up to Daniel. They were finally back to collecting data, with no more concern about wrecks for now. No sharks. No weirdness. Just science, which is why he'd come down here in the first place.

Once he and Mbeke were safely back onboard with their gear stowed away carefully, Chris sat down on the back gunwale to get a drink and warm up a bit in the sun. The ocean was a chilly fifty-two degrees Fahrenheit.

The boat tied up alongside was clearly a dive boat. And from the looks of the people on the back deck, they were tourists. He looked up to Daniel and nodded toward the divers, "What's going on over here, Daniel?"

"What?" Daniel looked up as he prepped his gear for the next dive. "Oh, you mean the dive boat? Kathryn has been encouraging ecotourism in the MPAs. She wants to bring more attention to NAMARI and its efforts to manage the marine environment. They're tied up to us for a few minutes."

"So where are they from?"

"I think that boat came all the way down from Cape Town. The owner/operator knows Kathryn and heard about the wreck that you and

Mbeke found. Nothing satisfies tourists like a wreck dive, eh? Even an old fishing boat."

"We have that conversation back in California all the time. One group wants to add wrecks along the coast to increase diving tourism, because like you said, divers love their wrecks. The other group wonders why people can't be satisfied with the incredible natural beauty."

"Where do you come down on that one, Chris?" Kara stepped out of the cabin in her wetsuit.

"I guess I come down somewhere in between the two extremes. I like a good wreck dive as much as anyone, but we probably don't need them everywhere."

Daniel laughed. "Are you running for office or something back home and not telling me about it? That answer, I think you Americans would say, was 'non-committal' in the extreme!"

Chris smiled at Daniel's use of Americanisms. Daniel had come to California several years prior on an exchange program with the university. While in Monterey, Daniel had made an effort to attend almost every meeting Chris went to. The guy had been a sponge for information, Chris remembered, so it was no surprise that Daniel was pulling out these little cherubs.

"You've been watching too much Netflix," Chris said.

Mbeke climbed up out of the hold where he was checking on the engines and asked, "Who's watching too much Netflix?" Looking toward Kara and Daniel he added, "I can barely get it to function on my computer in the lab. It's killing me."

Chris joined Kara and Daniel in their laughter, picturing big Mbeke trying to get Netflix to work. Looking out toward the dive boat he asked, "I wonder where they're from?"

Daniel, still chuckling, said, "Why don't you ask them?"

Chris, moving on, clapped his hands together loudly, "Okay! Is the B-team ready to get in the water? Let's get this show rolling."

Once Kara and Daniel were in the water, Chris and Mbeke sat down to copy the morning dive's data from the waterproof paper attached to their dive slates into notebooks. Later, when they returned to shore, the data would be uploaded to an online database, making three copies of data collected for every dive—the dive sheet used underwater, the hard copy in the notebook, and the digital copy.

Chris knew from experience that the absence of adequate back-up copies could spell disaster. He'd heard the oft repeated phrase that "if it isn't written down, it didn't happen," and modified it for his research team to be "if it isn't written down in three places, it isn't research."

Thinking that Mbeke might be opening up a bit, Chris said, "You were solid out there today. You must be feeling better after our little adventure with your tank and that shark."

"Yeah."

"How's your dissertation research going?"

"Pretty good."

"Think it's going to rain?"

"Maybe."

Chris had noticed earlier that Mbeke was pretty quiet unless either Kara or Daniel was around. With his friends around, Mbeke was much more forthcoming. Not unlike Mac, Chris thought.

Giving up on conversation with Mbeke, Chris walked over the starboard gunwale and surveilled the group of divers on the other boat. There were thirteen of them in various states of preparation for their next dive. Four likely Europeans huddled together at the stern speaking what sounded like German to each other. Another four sitting forward of the Europeans looking dower, sat quietly with all their gear ready.

Chris guessed that they were locals. The five closest to Chris looked, and sounded, like Americans. He made eye contact with one of the divers closest to him, a large red-headed man squeezing into a wetsuit that didn't entirely fit him. "Howdy. Where are you guys from?"

The man, who appeared to be in his forties, answered, "My wife, daughter, and I are all from the United States. Colorado, to be exact. Those two guys next to us are from New Jersey, and Mary over there is from San Francisco, I think. You sound like you're American."

"Yep. Name's Chris."

"I'm Tom. This is my daughter's graduation trip. She's always wanted to dive in South Africa. We came down to dive with white sharks at Seal Island, but we couldn't get a reservation until day after tomorrow. So here we are."

"That sounds great. What are you guys planning today, Tom?"

"I think we're about to move over to a different mooring and dive on a wreck. Everyone is pretty excited. What are you doing out here?"

"I'm here from California for six months of research working with NAMARI in this marine protected area."

"Ah, you're a scientist."

"Yep."

Hearing that Chris was a scientist, Tom's daughter perked up. "Have you been diving at Seal Island?"

"Not yet, but I expect I will before I go home." He nodded toward Mbeke, and then continued in a quieter voice, "My colleagues don't want me to go. Too touristy, they say. But there's no way I'm going home without diving there."

"Have you seen any white sharks around here?" the young woman asked.

"Oh, they're around. Think about it this way, even if you don't see them, you can be sure they've seen you."

One of the New Jersey divers interrupted. "What gas are you diving over there?"

Stifling a sarcastic response, Chris replied, "We dive either air or NITROX. Nothing too sexy." Years before, when Chris worked as a divemaster on a charter boat in Massachusetts, he frequently had to put up with divers from New Jersey coming up to dive off Cape Cod. It wasn't only that they brought too much gear with them, or that all they talked about was the deep diving they did back in New Jersey that had bothered him. It was the way they tried to make everyone else in the boat feel inferior.

"We've got NITROX in our main tanks, and HELIOX in our bailout bottles."

"Sounds great," Chris replied.

"We're planning to penetrate the wreck and record the entire effort on video. We want to be the first divers to penetrate."

"That sounds awesome," Chris said, thinking the exact opposite.

He looked over to Mary and asked, "Are you from SF?"

"I am," she replied. "You?"

"Carmel."

"Well, we're practically neighbors," Mary said, smiling as she continued to prepare her SCUBA rig.

The captain of the dive boat powered up the engines. Chris and Mbeke helped toss over the bow and stern lines that had held the two boats together.

"We'll probably be working on the boat when we return to port," Chris said to Mary and Tom. "When you come back into Simon's Town, find me on the boat and perhaps we can all go out to dinner. I've only been here three weeks, but a little interaction with home might be fun."

"We'll do that!" Tom said.

Chris watched as the dive boat motored over to an adjacent mooring and tied off. Ten minutes later the first divers were in the water. Chris noted that it wasn't the New Jersey divers leading the way. He smiled and then returned to working with Mbeke.

Thirty-five minutes later they finished processing the data sheets. Daniel and Kara were still underwater. Mbeke got up, walked out of the cabin onto the back deck, and stretched. He turned to say something to Chris when suddenly the water around the other dive boat erupted in a huge explosion.

25

It took several seconds for the waves created by the explosion to reach NAMARI's boat. In that time Chris had watched the dive boat capsize in the churning surface waters created by the blast. It was now completely "turtled," sitting upside down in the water.

Both Chris and Mbeke ran to the gunwale to look for Daniel and Kara. Looking at his watch, Chris noted that they should be at the surface any minute.

"Mbeke, call this in to the Coast Guard, Chris yelled, motioning toward the wheelhouse. "Tell them at least eight people were in the water at the time of the explosion. We'll respond as soon as we've accounted for our own divers."

While Chris scanned the surface around the boat looking for any sign of Daniel and Kara, his mind raced through what little he remembered from a recent physics lecture on the effect of underwater explosions on the human body. He knew that, in general, an underwater explosion was considerably more dangerous than an explosion on land. The pressure wave from a blast travels much faster through water than it does through air due to the increased density. He remembered that the main problem for humans came from the fact that the human body had essentially the same viscosity as the surrounding water. This meant that while skin and tissue might repel some of the force of a blast in air, a pressure wave underwater would travel straight through tissue, wreaking havoc on all internal organs.

This, Chris knew, did not bode well for the divers closest to the explosion. But there was always a chance that the blast wave had been dissipated somewhat by variable densities in seawater and/or redirected by seafloor topography. Thinking of the high-relief rocky reef below the vessel, he hoped that his friends had been near the seafloor when the explosion happened and had thus been protected by the reef.

Chris could hear Mbeke talking to the Coast Guard in the wheel-house, but he could also hear the faint sounds of air bubbles reaching the surface. Moving over to the starboard rail, he breathed a huge sigh of relief as he looked down to see both divers slowly ascending through the last ten feet of water. Thirty seconds later they were both at the surface.

Pulling off his mask, Daniel looked up at Chris and asked, "What the hell was that?"

"I don't know. There was a large explosion under that dive boat," Chris said, using his thumb to point over his shoulder. "It's upside down, and I've seen no signs of life."

"Oh my god," Kara said. "I counted thirteen people in the water over there."

"I know," Chris replied. "Let's get you guys on board, and then we'll see if we can help. Hand me your fins." Turning toward Daniel, he asked, "Were you guys down on the reef?"

"Yes," Daniel answered, as he passed his fins to Chris after Kara. "I guess we got lucky."

"Very lucky," Kara echoed, now on board. "My father was an underwater demolitions expert for much of his career. He admitted to me only recently that he lived in constant fear of even the slightest underwater explosion." Looking over toward the capsized dive boat she added, "I don't see any signs of life."

Mbeke came out of the wheelhouse. "The Coast Guard is sending a vessel and a helicopter, but neither will be here for at least thirty minutes."

Chris, who was still in his wetsuit from his earlier dive, said, "I'm going back in."

"You're *what*?" Daniel asked. "Chris, we have no idea what happened over there. There could be more explosions at any second. It's just too dangerous."

"Daniel, of course it's dangerous. And the odds of finding anyone alive at this point are almost nil. But we can't just sit here and twiddle our thumbs. Let's move the boat over there. I'll jump in the water." He paused for a second, before continuing, "Kara can come with me. You and Mbeke can check out the boat and report to the Coast Guard when they arrive."

Chris knew Daniel was struggling with the difficult situation into which Chris had just put him. He was in charge of this team; sending anyone back in the water was fraught with peril.

Daniel shook his head a couple of times and then snapped into action. "Okay. Let's get you in the water. Mbeke, pull us off the mooring and move us over to the dive boat. Kara, switch out your tank. I'll pull out the oxygen and first aid kits in case you find anyone alive down there."

26

Chris could tell without turning his head that Kara was beside him as he swam through the murk along the seafloor, because the strong waterproof light she carried was illuminating the seafloor right in front of him. Both of them were on edge as they explored the debris field created by the explosion and he was glad Kara was there. The already poor visibility along the bottom had not been improved by the explosion, but it was possible to swim above the cloud of sediment to obtain a longer view. That is how they first noticed a cloud of bubbles coming from the far side of the wreck.

Swimming quickly over the remnants of the wreck they could see the consequences of the explosion. The main cabin had disintegrated, but the back deck was strangely intact, resting on the bottom at the edge of a large crater in the sand. Chris noted the presence of small fish that had already returned to the area. These species survived by picking at invertebrates and algae. The explosion would have exposed much of the wreck and seafloor that hadn't been accessible to scavengers prior, and they were moving in to see what they could find.

But Chris also noticed two other things that caught his eye—a ladder mounted on the wreck's stern that he hadn't seen the first time they dove on it and a large rocky outcropping adjacent to the wreck that had not been there before. Missing a ladder was one thing, Chris thought, but where did that reef outcropping come from?

Cresting over the reef in pursuit of the bubbles' origin, Chris and Kara discovered three divers on the seafloor. The closest two were both male, one extremely heavyset who looked like Tom, and the other Chris didn't recognize. Chris immediately moved toward Tom, while Kara checked the other. Neither of the men was breathing. Chris could see the remnant of Tom's regulator mouthpiece still in his mouth. It looked as though he must have bit down on the mouth-piece at the moment of the blast, biting it completely off. The blast had also knocked Tom's mask and right fin off. His underwater camera, its housing crushed by the explosion but somehow still positively buoyant, hovered above his body connected to his wrist by a nylon lanyard.

Tom's lifeless eyes stared back at Chris. Thin spirals of blood, which appeared black at this depth, extended from each of his nostrils. Images of Tom alive, dutifully helping his wife and daughter prepare for their dive, flashed through Chris's mind. That had been only half an hour ago.

Looking toward Kara, Chris could see she was finding the other man to be in a similar condition. He indicated to her using hand signals that he was moving to the third diver.

The woman was lying on her back on the sand. Chris recognized her as Mary, not Tom's wife as he initially expected. Her regulator was still in her mouth and as she breathed the subtle change in buoyancy rocked her slowly from side to side on her tank.

Approaching Mary carefully, Chris rested his gloved hand on her shoulder and gently nudged her. To Chris's surprise, she opened her eyes and looked up at him. One of her eyes was bloodshot, while the pupil was dilated and unfocused in the second. But her mask was on and she was breathing, which gave Chris hope.

Chris made the okay sign in front of Mary's mask, followed by the thumbs up sign indicating that they were going to take her to the surface. Receiving no response, he did a quick visual check of the rest of her body. There were no obvious signs of injury, though Chris knew that any injuries from the blast were likely internal. Mary's gauge indicated that she still had half a tank of air, which would be plenty to get her safely to the surface.

As he and Kara slowly lifted Mary off the seafloor and began the slow ascent to the surface, Chris scanned the area in all directions in the hopes of spotting additional air bubbles. He saw none.

27

"It wasn't the same wreck," Chris said, pacing around the hospital cafeteria the next afternoon.

In the flurry of activity following Chris and Kara's ascent to the surface the day before, no one had time to discuss what they'd seen. The Coast Guard had evacuated Mary, along with Daniel, Kara, and Chris, by helicopter, leaving two crew to assist Mbeke in bringing the NAMARI boat back to port while the search and rescue team set about recovering the other missing divers. Because all of them had just been underwater, they were not supposed to fly for twelve hours. But the helicopter flew just above the sea surface to avoid creating any additional problems for them.

Kathryn and Claudia had arrived from NAMARI with the news that the bodies of all but two of the missing divers had been recovered by sundown the day before. A mangled BCD and tank found near the remnants of the wreck lead the Coast Guard to believe that the missing buddy team had probably been on the wreck when it exploded.

"What are you saying, Chris?" Kathryn asked, her eyes tracking Chris's steps back and forth. "I don't understand."

"This is going to sound crazy, but I think there are two wrecks down there, very close together," replied Chris, slowing down briefly to emphasize his point. "The wreck Kara and I swam over last week was different than the wreck that exploded yesterday. Similar, yes, but different."

"What was different?" Claudia asked.

"Yesterday I noticed that the back deck was different. The stern gunwale was intact and there was a ladder hanging over the side. The stern had collapsed on the other wreck. I recall that specifically because we had swum directly to the stern to see if we could find evidence of the vessel's name."

"You're sure of this?" Kathryn asked.

"Absolutely. And then there's the reef. The rocky outcropping that looks to have saved the woman's life yesterday wasn't present when Kara and I surveyed the wreck last week. It was tall enough to shield her partially from the blast. I'd remember reef that tall if we'd seen it before."

"Two wrecks?" Claudia asked. "I don't recall seeing a second wreck in the sonar imagery that MDK was analyzing. I wish he were here to discuss."

"I looked at that topographic map, too, and didn't see a second wreck. But it is possible that the high relief rocky reef in the area simply masked the second wreck from the sonar," Kathryn said.

"By the way, Michael de Klerk's family has filed a missing person report. No one has any idea where he went."

"He's missing?" Chris asked.

Kathryn shook her head. "No sign of him in the past two weeks. His mother is understandably distraught. But can we take a step back for a minute? I'm losing track of all these wrecks."

"Absolutely."

"Okay. Let's start with what we know: Last week you and Mbeke were near a wreck when his tank exploded."

"Yes."

"Then several days ago you and Kara surveyed a wreck."

"That's right."

"And then yesterday a wreck blew up."

Chris nodded.

"Now you're saying that there are two wrecks. Are you saying the wreck you and Mbeke saw was different from the wreck that blew up, the wreck you and Kara dove on, or both?"

The question gave Chris pause. "I don't know," he answered after a few seconds. "We were only on the wreck very briefly before Mbeke's tank valve exploded. But when Kara and I approached the wreck, I remember thinking that it looked different. The more I think about it now, the more I am convinced it was a different wreck."

"So which wreck blew up?" asked Claudia.

"I think it was the first site, the one Mbeke and I visited. Where *are* Daniel and Mbeke? I think we need to talk to them to see if they can confirm my own recollections."

"I spoke to Daniel this morning," Kathryn answered. "But I don't know where he is now. I expected him to be here. Mbeke is still talking with the Coast Guard."

The three of them sat quietly considering these new revelations, until a hospital administrator approached Kathryn. The man looked grave, and Chris anticipated what he was going to say.

"I'm sorry to report that the young woman has died of her injuries. Our doctors indicate it was a miracle she survived as long as she did.

"I'm sorry to report this sad news," he continued. "The family of the victim has been notified and I figured you would want to know. The hospital is handling all press inquiries."

"Thank you," Kathryn answered. Chris could see that both she and Claudia were visibly shaken by this news.

"Thirteen people dead," Kathryn said to no one in particular. "Thirteen people. I invited them to dive on the wreck. They would have never known about it had I not shared it with them. I thought it was such a great PR opportunity to have the public engaged with the MPA."

"You couldn't have known that this would happen," Claudia offered, placing her hand on Kathryn's forearm.

"Perhaps not. But it doesn't change the fact that I sent thirteen people to their deaths."

Chris was listening to Kathryn and Claudia's exchange with increasing concern. He knew from direct personal experience what it felt like to have situations like this spiral out of control. He also reflected on the email he'd sent the afternoon before, immediately after the helicopter had brought them back to Cape Town: *Mac. I think you'd better come down to Cape Town ASAP. Please bring the mini-ROV and console. And I think you'd better get Hendrix and team mobilized as well. I've got a very bad feeling about this. C.*

Mac's response, "Copy that," had been immediate. It was followed approximately twelve hours later with: *En route through Heathrow. Should be on ground in CT by 1600 local time. Hendrix & team already in Africa for some reason. Expect contact shortly. Mac out.*

Mac's use of twenty-four-hour time meant that he expected to land in Cape Town around 4:00 p.m., which was less than an hour away. Chris breathed a little bit easier knowing that his close friend and colleague would shortly be on site. He and Mac and had been through a lot together over the years. More than once Mac's training as a Navy SEAL had served them both.

And then there was Hendrix, Mac's former colleague in the SEALs. Chris had been pretty skeptical of Hendrix at first. It was difficult to see through the sarcasm and vague admissions to understand exactly what Hendrix and his team did. But it soon became clear that the private "security consultants" were invaluable in difficult situations. Indeed, Chris was convinced that he would not have survived the recent events in Carmel had Hendrix not been involved.

Chris stood up to stretch and walked over to the cafeteria's buffet to see what he could scrounge up to eat, since he hadn't eaten anything since breakfast. Grabbing a banana and two chocolate chip cookies, he was moving toward the cashier when the two double doors at the far end of the cafeteria opened. Chris immediately recognized the two men walking in through the door, one tall and black and the other shorter and Caucasian, as the two he'd seen in the elevator at NAMARI the previous week.

The black man scanned the cafeteria before his eyes settled on Chris. Starring at each other across a crowded sea of cafeteria diners, Chris could see that the man also recognized him. Time seemed to stop. Then the men quickly turned and hurried back out the door.

This was no coincidence.

Thinking about the thirteen people that had died such a violent death in the explosion, Chris quickly placed his food on a nearby counter and ran toward the door.

28

The large double doors lead to the hospital's north stairwell. By the time Chris made it across the crowded cafeteria, the two men were gone. Guessing that their first impulse would be to escape the hospital, he quickly descended the six flights to the lobby. As he went his mind raced through the possibilities. He had no idea who these two men were, but seeing them both at NAMARI as well as the hospital was strongly suggestive; and their response to seeing Chris was further evidence that something was afoot.

Recalling his failure in Carmel to put together the loose strands of a criminal narrative until it was too late, Chris was not going to let that happen again. He was about to catch an elevator back to the cafeteria to get Kathryn's help in obtaining the hospital's security camera footage, when Frank Donagan walked in through the hospital's revolving glass door.

"Dr. Black, how interesting to see you again," Donagan said. "And so soon, too." He didn't remove his sunglasses.

"What are you doing here?" Chris couldn't conceal his surprise.

"Several of the divers who died, including the woman that you rescued, were American tourists. I'm here on their behalf to try and better understand what happened."

Chris stood still, staring at Donagan. "I know. I met several of them before the dive. They were nice people. Nice, reasonable people on the trip of a lifetime. They didn't deserve this."

"What do you think happened, Dr. Black?"

"I don't know, Mr. Donagan. But I'd like to find out."

"Please, call me Frank. So you have no theories?"

Chris knew the cavalry was coming. Mac was now likely on the ground in Cape Town if his flight had arrived on schedule. Curiously, he'd had no contact from Hendrix, but he expected that to change soon. Hendrix had a flair for the dramatic.

He was unsure how much to discuss with Donagan, the self-described employee of the American embassy. Chris wondered what he'd learn if he went to the embassy asking to see Mr. Donagan. But he couldn't deny that he actually liked the guy. There was something about his affect that encouraged Chris to trust him.

"I just encountered two men upstairs in the cafeteria that I've seen before, last week at the NAMARI building. When they saw me they bolted. I came down the stairs quickly, but they were long gone."

"What did these two men look like?" Donagan asked. Chris thought he detected a slight change in Donagan's posture.

"One was a black guy, about my height. He looked dangerous. Carried a machete strapped to his leg. The other man was Caucasian. He was shorter and less imposing, but I still sensed a devious vibe. I was just about to go back upstairs to talk to Kathryn, the NAMARI director, to see if she can get access to the hospital security footage."

"Good impulse. I'll take care of that. How do you think these two men are involved? And why?"

"I have no idea how. And why? Just call it my sixth sense sharpened by experience with nefarious individuals."

Donagan gave him a probing look that seemed poised to challenge him, but then, much to Chris's surprise, he simply nodded. "Do you have any idea why an old shipwreck would blow up, killing thirteen people?"

"Nope. Maybe what blew up were unexploded munitions from some previous conflict? I know that kind of thing still happens. I've been diving on a WWI munitions ship off Cape Cod that still has phosphorus bombs in its hold. They are inactive while under water, but if you were to bring one to the surface, the bomb's reaction to exposure to air is very likely to result in an explosion. That has happened before."

"You've been down on the wreck, haven't you? Did it look like a munitions ship to you?"

"Good point. It didn't. It looked like a fishing vessel. Except . . ." As he said that, Chris recalled the round object he'd found by the wreck during his dive with Kara. It was sitting in his BCD pocket on the reserve boat.

"Except what? Anything you would like to share?"

"Not yet. But soon." Chris headed for the revolving door. "I've got to go check into something. Will you let me know how it goes with the security camera footage?"

"I will. But I would like to hear more of your thoughts on this situation, Dr. Black."

Now on his way out the door, Chris offered, "Yep. Be in touch soon."

29

Jacob Slovo and Pieter Jonker left the hospital immediately after seeing Chris Black in the cafeteria. They'd come to see what had happened to the single surviving diver of the explosion on the wreck, which they'd learned about through one of Slovo's connections on the dock.

Prior to that, they had been on Slovo's boat attempting to visit the wreck site. But the site was now occupied by South African Coast Guard vessel and a couple of other small boats. At least for the time being, it was going to be challenging to get down to the wreck.

"There is little doubt now that Black knows we're involved," Slovo said as they drove southwest toward Greyling's house. "I told both you and Greyling that rigging the wreck was a bad idea. Now we have thirteen dead tourists and a whole bunch of new interest in the wreck."

After parking in front of Greyling's house, Slovo had to follow Jonker, who had nearly jumped out of the car upon their arrival, into the house. Inside he found Jonker complaining to Greyling that Slovo had compromised the operation.

"He didn't let me go back up and take out Black at the NAMARI building, and we just lost another chance at the hospital."

Greyling, working through a deep, phlegmy cough, turned to Slovo. "Is this true, my little *kaffer*?"

Slovo responded by quickly drawing his machete out of its sheath and hacking nearly through Jonker's neck with a single stroke. Jonker's body dropped to the floor, his head now only loosely attached. Blood pooled on the old rug, darkening it even further.

Slovo turned toward Greyling slowly. "Go ahead. Call me *kaffer* again."

Greyling offered nothing but another phlegmy cough as two men emerged from the shadows behind him. Slovo had not known nor sensed that they were there. They both held pistols.

"I will call you whatever I damn well please, *kaffer*. Step out of line again and you'll be the one in a pool of blood." Slovo looked down at Jonker's body and the growing puddle.

"But I don't think we'll kill you just yet. Not just yet. You and your little knife could still prove useful," Greyling continued. "Jonker was right that we should kill Black. It should have been done already. My connections with NAMARI can get us back on the site and back on track. But we need to remove Black from the picture."

"Who will dive on the wreck?" Slovo asked.

"You leave that to me. Find and kill Black. Then wait for my call. I will have divers on your boat within twenty-four hours."

Slovo was tired of dealing with this old man and his ridiculous schemes to recover gold from the wreck. He could see no way that this was possible at this point. There would just be too much attention after the explosion. It would be much cleaner, and safer for him, if he just killed everyone in the house right now, then killed Black. Then he'd be clear to find a new project with a higher probability of success.

Slovo gripped his machete handle even tighter as he noticed Greyling nod to the two men. They immediately leveled their cocked pistols at Slovo. "Your choice, *kaffer*. Die now or die later and a great deal richer."

Slovo, though seething, opted for later and richer and left to find the guys to help him kill Chris Black.

30

Chris Black arrived at the dock to find his childhood friend Mac already waiting for him aboard the boat talking to Mbeke. "I can barely straighten my legs after almost twenty-four hours in a coach class seat. And for God's sake, what time is it anyway? What time zone are we in?"

"I missed you, too," Chris replied, moving past the grumpiness. "And it's time to figure out what's going on around here."

Robert 'Mac' Johnson was a physical and temperamental counterpoint to his close friend Chris. He wore his hair a bit longer, in a small pirate-like ponytail, which usually poked out from under one of Mac's many baseball caps. Where Chris was tall and longer-limbed, Mac was a compact five foot nine inches and a dense one hundred and ninety pounds. His ponytail and perpetual smirk gave him the appearance of youth, though he was the same age as Chris. And where Chris was quick to start up a discussion with a stranger, Mac was far less conversational, even when among friends.

While Chris had pursued an academic career from the beginning, Mac had turned to engineering only after being forced to leave the Navy SEALs following an injury. They'd been working together since Mac had been hired at the CMEx.

"Mbeke was bringing me up to speed on the explosion yesterday," Mac said. "The ROV's down in the hold and ready to go. Not a lot of daylight left today. What's our dive plan?"

"We'll get to that in a minute," Chris said. "First let me check something out."

He went down into the hold and emerged a couple of minutes later with the object he'd found on the wreck during his dive with Kara. The night before he'd been reviewing recent events in his mind when he'd realized that he'd completely forgotten about it.

"Mbeke, do we have a small hammer or something on board?" He also tossed Mac an energy bar he'd had in his backpack.

"Yes!" replied Mbeke, enthusiastically. Perhaps Mac was actually having a good influence on someone for a change, Chris thought. "In fact," Mbeke continued, "Dr. Brody left some of his archaeological tools on board after this last expedition. There is a small ball-peen hammer in that kit."

Mbeke went below decks and returned quickly with the hammer he had described.

Chris moved over the sorting table scientists used to sift through samples and placed the round object on the table.

"What do you have there?" asked Mac while devouring the energy bar.

"I'm not sure. It could be nothing. I found it next to the wreck when Kara and I dove on it. Its round shape struck me as odd."

"Ah yes," Mac said. "I've seen this movie too. Next you crack that object open to find a Spanish doubloon at its center and we all retire early. Oh, and I get to go home with Jacqueline Bisset this time."

Chris was glad to have Mac back at his side.

The first two strikes at the object produced no visible change.

"You're not one of those archaeological weenies," Mac offered. "Put some muscle into it for God's sake." Mbeke laughed.

Chris swung the hammer with a great deal more strength the third time and the object split in half. The split revealed an impossibly brilliant gold coin that reflected the setting sun in their eyes.

All three of the men were briefly speechless. Chris tapped the lower half of the coin with the hammer one more time to remove the remaining bit of accumulated corrosion. He then dipped the coin in the water of a nearby holding tank and set it on the table.

"That's no Spanish doubloon," Mac said. "Is that an antelope?"

"Not exactly," Chris looked at the image of something like an antelope engraved on the face of the coin. "I think that's a springbok; a type of antelope here in South Africa. Is that what I think it is, Mbeke?"

"It's a Krugerrand," Mbeke said. "It's South Africa's gold coin; nearly pure 24 carat gold. When I was in grade school it was *the* gold standard for most of the world."

"Is that from Apartheid?" asked Mac.

"Yes," answered Mbeke. "It was created in the sixties as a way to encourage private ownership of gold."

"What do you mean?"

"Regular people weren't allowed to own gold directly, and South Africa had a lot of gold. So they came up with a way to sell gold to private citizens around the world."

"How much do you think it's worth?" Mac asked.

"We can check that easily," replied Mbeke, reaching for his smart phone. "But it is probably worth maybe $1,500 U.S. dollars right now."

"I've got a very bad feeling about this." Mac looked at Chris. "Didn't you come down here looking for rest and recovery?"

31

Chris drove while Mac watched for anyone tailing them. They'd left Mbeke on the boat where the guards Kathryn had placed would keep him safe. As he navigated the roads back to his house in Kommetjie, he reflected on his recent encounters with crooked cops back home in Carmel. A pattern was starting to form in the back of his mind that seemed familiar; a series of ostensibly unrelated events, followed by a fateful discovery, all against a backdrop of potential betrayal from someone close.

"Are you going to bring me up to speed?" asked Mac.

Chris did so as he drove, and the two discussed the merits of bringing in additional people into what Mac deemed the "circle of trust." Kathryn clearly needed to be informed, but Chris wanted to have a better handle on exactly what was going on before approaching her. Daniel, Chris's best option for connecting to NAMARI, was still nowhere to be found.

"What about this Claudia person?" Mac asked. "If I understand it correctly, she is precisely the type of middle-management person we could use at this point. Not too important to be hamstrung by procedure and not a low-level functionary."

"I think we can bring Claudia into the circle, but . . ."

"Wait just a minute. Don't say another word. Has the infamous Chris Black charm been working its magic?"

Chris didn't want to get Mac going on the subject of Claudia, so he left details of the strange situation for later. "Oh, I think you'll like Claudia. She is very, shall we say, straightforward. She's not shy."

"Interesting," Mac said. "Okay, so Claudia is in. Daniel is in, too, whenever he comes back up on radar."

"Right. And there's this guy from the embassy we should probably include. He keeps popping up at moments that suggest to me something else is going on. And I think he can help with local law enforcement. Or at least, he has insinuated such in the past."

"A guy from the embassy? That sounds dubious, but I'll take your word for it. The embassy guy is in."

"And where is Hendrix? Don't tell him this, but I'm starting to like having his particular skill set around."

"Oh, I'm sure he already knows that, or at least he assumes it's the case. Hendrix is the Keyser Soze of the security world; he's a figment of your imagination right up until he's not. And then you can't get rid of him. As he demonstrated in the Carmel Canyon Incident, he clearly likes you. I'm sure he'll be along."

"Is that what we're calling it now? The Carmel Canyon Incident?"

"Would you prefer the Adventure of the Red Barrels? Or maybe the Case of the Toxic Sludge? I've got a million of them."

"I'm sure you do."

32

Jacob Slovo left Greyling's dilapidated mansion in a rage. He'd been ready to die on the spot. It would have been worth it to cut up that phlegmy old racist, he thought, and then he would have been reunited with his wife and daughter. But the possibility of getting the gold from the wreck, however remote, helped keep his anger in check.

Slovo had gone straight to the marina in Simon's Town to meet with the three men Greyling had loaned him earlier for the interrogation of the NAMARI computer analyst. Like the old geezer himself, they were racist bastards. But Slovo was able to work through that given their obvious toughness and the fact that he didn't have any other good options.

Sitting in the wheelhouse of the boat on which Michael de Klerk had made his final trip, one of the three thugs said, "Listen, blackie. We don't care about politics, okay? We just want our money. If a blackie can help get us our money, we don't care, okay?"

"Fine. What did de Klerk tell you?" Slovo asked.

"Nothing. The little man did nothing but throw up on my deck and shit himself before we tossed him to the sharkies."

"Bullshit. He must have told you something."

"Boss didn't care if he told us anything," said another one of the three. "Boss said he has another way to get the information. Another spy. A better spy. So we didn't care, either."

This made Slovo pause. He'd already met with one other NAMARI member being blackmailed by Greyling. And he knew how that person had been compromised. But was there a third source in the picture?

Access to the NAMARI research vessel was protected by local authorities. The men explained that two of the NAMARI employees were on the boat, but that Black and another man they did not recognize had left earlier in Black's vehicle. Slovo was sure that getting past the local police would be no problem. But getting on the boat was not a priority at this point. Black was.

"What do you want us to do, blackie?" one of the men asked.

Pulling out his machete, Slovo said, "The next one of you calls me blackie loses an arm. You understand?" Slovo could tell that, though wary of the machete, the men were not too impressed by threats.

"I want you to go to this address and kill the yank and whoever is with him. No big plans. No trips out to the sharks. Just walk in the door and kill whoever's in the house."

Each of the three men nodded.

"He's just a scientist," Slovo added. "Should be no problem. Kill him, then come back here."

Slovo could tell that the men didn't like taking orders from him. He took a measured step towards them and with a smile he added, "I'll want a full report."

33

When Chris pulled through the gate to his place, Claudia was waiting outside, sitting on a bench in the setting sun. He'd called her from the road. Chris had also placed a call to the number on Frank Donagan's card and left a message.

"So that's Claudia, eh?" Mac asked before they got out of the SUV. "I stand by my 'interesting' comment. Also, don't let me forget to tell you about what's going on with Abby."

"Peter's beat you to it, I'm afraid," Chris said.

"Did he tell you about the Galapagos trip they'll be taking together on the *MacGreggor*?"

"Yes. I could almost feel his glee coming through the phone. I don't know what you guys are expecting me to say. I'm fine with Abby doing whatever she thinks she needs to do. Everyone just needs to calm down and move on. There are more interesting things to worry about."

"Yeah, okay. I'm sorry. I've just got nothing going myself, so I guess I'm living vicariously through your relationship travails."

"My travails?"

"Yes, your travails. Plus, without Margaret around, who's going to keep you emotionally centered?"

"I can't think of anyone better suited to manage my emotional health than you."

"Excellent! We at least agree on that. Now let's get out and meet Claudia."

The three large plastic tubes resting on Claudia's lap indicated that she'd brought with her hard copies of the latest and greatest versions of the topographic maps for the area around the wreck site. Though everything was available digitally at this point, in a throwback to earlier in his career, Chris still preferred to have maps spread out on the table in front of him.

After the requisite introductions, and more fun at Chris's expense than, in his mind, was warranted for the situation, the three of them sat down to consider the topographic maps in earnest.

"This is the area where we've been working on the reef with the highest resolution maps," Chris indicated as he was pointing to the map. "When Daniel mentioned that the wreck that had shown up on this new map, we simply set a course from the mooring line here toward the wreck. It was pretty easy to find."

Mac looked at Claudia, then at Chris. Putting his finger on the fairly clear lines of a wreck on the seafloor, he asked, "So is this the wreck you found? The wreck that was blown up? The same? Or neither? What is it that you think is happening exactly?"

"I am certain that there are two wrecks down there, and that I've been on both of them," Chris said emphatically. "Given that, I think the wreck visible on the map here is the wreck where Mbeke and I dove in the midst of these high relief rocky outcroppings here. That's the wreck that exploded.

"When Kara and I dove, we were pushed off course by a bottom current, which I think put us about here; about one-hundred and fifty feet to the south over predominantly sandy habitat."

Pointing again, Chris continued, "If you stand back from the map a bit and squint, doesn't that oval-shaped rise above the seafloor look like it might be a wreck right there?"

"Maybe," Mac said. "But I believe in Bigfoot, so clearly I'll believe just about anything."

Claudia let out a brief guffaw in response to that comment, giving rise to general laughter all around. Chris noted that she was not saying much but was following the conversation very closely. He wondered how she would respond to the next part of the story, which was almost entirely conjectured on his part.

"In all seriousness," Mac added. "I am more than willing to buy the two-wreck-theory. You've convinced me. And further, that is something we can confirm quite easily tomorrow, either on SCUBA or with the ROV."

"Definitely," Chris said. "We'll need to do both, and here's why. I think that there's a trove of Krugerrands down there on that wreck."

"That is based on what? Your finding a single coin?"

"That, and the fact that when Kara and I dove on the wreck the first time the bow was set deeper in the sand, and the stern protruded out further above the seafloor, than you would expect for a wreck that had lots of time to settle to the bottom. I couldn't figure it out at the time, but I think the bow is weighted down by something extremely heavy."

"Like a lot of gold krugerrands?"

"I think so. During our dive I got a good look into the hold and saw at least fifteen barrels full of something heavy. That was what kept the wreck oriented the way that it is."

"Barrels again? You've got to be kidding me."

"You're telling me. But this time, I think those barrels are filled with Krugerrands."

Before either Mac or Claudia had a chance to reply to Chris's theory, the front door of the flat burst open and two large men rushed in.

Chris and Mac were on their feet in an instant. But just as quickly it became clear that wasn't necessary.

Hendrix—Chris had never learned his first name—followed the men in with his weapon drawn, leveled at the men in front of him. He was shorter than Chris, but gained a few inches based on toughness alone. His head was no longer shaved, as he sported thick black hair and a matching beard. His neck was permanently scarred from what appeared to be a failed hanging.

Hendrix usually wore sunglasses with reflective lenses, so one rarely got a direct look at his eyes. But during the few moments that Chris had seen Hendrix without his glasses the previous year, he'd looked right into the eyes of a warrior. Sure, there was kindness and mirth visible from time to time, but when Hendrix wasn't directly engaging him, Chris could see Hendrix constantly taking the measure of everyone and everything within his cone of vision. If Hendrix and his crew hadn't helped to find Chris when he'd been taken hostage during the *Carmel Canyon Incident*, Chris knew he'd have been dead.

"Dr. Black! It is good to see you," Hendrix said. "Sorry to make such a dramatic entrance."

"That's what we call a non-apology apology."

"Johnson, you'll get yours later," Hendrix continued, unfazed. "From the moment we arrived in country we picked up some chatter that you were being targeted. So, we wanted to hang back and see what developed."

"Chatter? Targeted by whom?" Chris asked.

"We'll get to that. These two guys, as well as a third lying out in your driveway, were waiting for you to come out. But the jokers failed to realize that *we* were waiting for *them*."

Without speaking, Mac took large plastic zip ties from Hendrix and bound the hands of each of the men behind them. They were both

Caucasian and very muscular. When they refused to sit, Mac delivered a well-placed kick to the back of their knees that achieved the same result.

One of the men spoke through clenched teeth, "Fuckin Yanks."

Ignoring him, Chris queried, "What is going on outside?"

"My team has secured the area. No one else is coming in tonight. The deceased will be removed shortly, if he isn't already gone. Your new friend has seen to that. He will join us in a minute, by the way."

"My new friend?"

"Dr. Black! We can't keep meeting like this!" Chris turned to see Frank Donagan walk through the door.

34

Chris Black had learned long ago from his dad, a former fighter pilot in Vietnam, that in the midst of battle you can't let the rapidly accumulating stimuli overwhelm you. Rather than fixate on any one new piece of information, you need to achieve an appropriate level of psychological distance in order to keep the big picture in focus. This is particularly true, his dad had noted, when the new information is coming in very quickly.

This approach had served Chris well many times in the field as circumstances threatened to spiral out of control on research projects. And it served him now as Hendrix and Donagan made their dramatic appearances.

It was immediately clear that Chris's small granny flat was not going to work for what needed to be done next. Donagan suggested against calling the local authorities right away in favor of some more direct interrogation of the two captured thugs. "We don't yet know who's involved, and to what extent."

Hendrix agreed, which neither Chris nor Mac found surprising. Given that Chris, Mac, and Claudia still held positions in the real world, and consequently couldn't simply disappear in the event of legal problems, it was decided that they would relocate to the main house while the interrogations occurred in Chris's flat. The owners of the main house had left the keys for Chris—just in case, as they had said—though he doubted seriously that they'd had this type of situation in mind.

Claudia and Chris moved into the main house first, with one of Hendrix's men stationed at the front door. As soon as the door closed Claudia turned to Chris and hugged him hard, not releasing for what seemed like an unnecessarily long time.

Enjoying the embrace, Chris hugging her back with equal vigor. "I'm so sorry that you have to be involved with this. I know that that was intense. How are you doing?"

Claudia kept her face buried in Chris's neck for a little while longer before she came up for air. Chris expected to see fear, sadness, confusion, or some combination of the three, but what he saw in her eyes instead was steely determination. In that moment, for reasons he wouldn't be able to articulate until later, Claudia went up in his estimation immeasurably.

"Where did all these guys come from?" she asked.

"Mac is one of my closest friends dating back to childhood, but he is also a close colleague. I asked him to fly down here to help figure out exactly what is going on. Hendrix is a colleague of Mac's from their days in the military. He's proven to be invaluable in these kinds of situations."

"What kinds of situations?"

"Challenging situations? I guess that describes it. I asked for Hendrix to help without knowing the full extent of the danger. And I'm glad that I did, for had his team not been on site when those thugs arrived things could have gone a very different way."

"As you know, I've heard stories around the office ever since you arrived about what happened to you back in California."

"Mac has taken to referring to it as the *Carmel Canyon Incident*."

"Whatever. I have to admit that some of that is what attracted me to you so quickly. Not the mythology that seems to surround you, but the simple fact you faced unbelievable threats to yourself, your friends, and your family, and you persevered." She frowned. "I just don't understand how you can do that. Persevere."

Chris released Claudia and sat down hard on the living room couch. "I'm not sure I can give you an easy answer that is any different than when we were down at the Cape of Good Hope. I had a conversation very much like this six months ago in the middle of that incident, and I didn't have an answer then, either."

Claudia sat down next to Chris on the couch. "I don't really expect an answer. I guess I'm just looking to understand where your strength comes from."

"Strength? Sometimes I don't feel very strong at all. My students speak of something called *Imposter Syndrome*. Do you know of it?"

Claudia shook her head. "I'm not sure that I do, though I can probably guess from the title."

"Right. It's basically the fear of being exposed as fraud, regardless of how accomplished one is. The students love to talk about it. The thing I keep reinforcing for them is that a) the syndrome doesn't stop when you reach some magical waypoint in your career, and b) you can't let the syndrome prevent you from moving forward."

"You sound like you're a good professor."

"Who knows? I'm probably a total fraud. All I know for sure is that I try to keep moving forward. And the strength? That comes from those around me. I'm not even sure I'd get out of bed in the morning if I didn't have exciting challenges to confront alongside my truly inspiring colleagues."

"Don't you ever want to give up, or maybe run away? I mean three huge guys just came to kill you? To kill you! That doesn't happen to most of us. Do you realize that?"

"Yeah, I get that. They tried. And I expect that they'll try again. And who knows, maybe they'll succeed the next time. But I'll tell you this, six months ago I was done with all of this. I never wanted to deal with bad guys ever again. But you know what?"

Chris stood up before proceeding. He was too animated to sit still. "Now I'm fucking *mad* again. They've put me back in touch with my inner demons, and I'm going make them pay for all of it—for killing those thirteen divers, for threatening us, for all the horrible things I'm sure that they've done to scores of other people along the way. They're going down."

He could feel Claudia's eyes upon him as he paced.

"That family from Colorado was just here to celebrate the daughter's graduation! They didn't deserve any of this. And unfortunately for whoever is doing this, it isn't just me that they're facing. I would never want to be on either Mac's or Hendrix's bad sides. Those guys are trained to bring the pain."

Chris stopped his rant and stood looking at Claudia. She steadily returned his gaze. Making eye contact with her was like nothing he'd ever experienced. She seemed to have a core of inner strength that eclipsed his.

"Chris, I . . ."

There was a hard wrap at the front door. Daniel Opperman walked in followed closely by Mac.

"Hendrix's team found this guy out front," Mac said pointing at Daniel, who looked from Claudia, to Mac, to Chris.

"Chris, what the hell is going on?"

35

It took Slovo several seconds to understand what he was seeing. He'd sent the three men to kill what they assumed was an unsuspecting Chris Black inside his house, along with his unnamed guest. Slovo remained up the hill above the neighborhood to monitor the situation and to report to Greyling once the job was done.

The plan was very simple. They would force their way into the undefended house and kill everyone inside. No discussion. No bargaining.

But the men had barely stepped foot in Black's driveway when they were taken down, with minimal effort, by a group of what appeared to be highly trained military who'd materialized out of nowhere.

One of Slovo's men looked to have been killed outright, while the other two were quickly disarmed and subdued.

Slovo, who'd been witness to the violent end of many people, had to appreciate the precision of the paramilitary team's actions. And it left him wondering, not without a tinge of admiration and respect, just who this Chris Black really was.

36

A half hour after Daniel arrived, the group convened in the living room of the main house, including Chris, Claudia, Mac, Daniel, Hendrix, and Donagan. An unspecified number of Hendrix's team remained outside to guard the perimeter. Chris first brought everyone up to speed on his theory of the two wrecks. Everyone then turned to Hendrix and Donagan to hear what they'd found from interrogating the two thugs.

Hendrix motioned toward Donagan and said, "I defer to my colleague with the greater experience in country."

"I don't think deference is your strong suit Hendrix, but I'll take what I can get." Donagan chuckled. "Unfortunately, we learned very little from the two men. They are hired functionaries working for someone name Greyling. Three weeks ago they were hired to abduct and interrogate a computer technician from NAMARI."

"Michael de Klerk," Daniel said flatly, putting the pieces together.

"That's right," Donagan replied. "They indicated that de Klerk had apparently talked openly at a night club about his job and the fact that he had recently identified a wreck inside the MPA using a high-resolution topographic map of the seafloor. The bartender asked de Klerk questions about the dimensions of the wreck and the habitat around it. De Klerk apparently talked himself up a bit too much. That led others to him, and these others paid de Klerk a 'large sum' for a flash drive with the wreck location and a detailed sonar image on it. He was told not to discuss that transaction, but apparently he did, at least with the bartender, anyway."

"Who's Greyling?" Chris asked.

"We don't know yet," Hendrix answered.

"But we'll find out," Donagan promised as he looked at Daniel and Claudia. "Do either of you have anything to contribute from the NAMARI end of things?"

Daniel spoke first. "I run the field operations, so I had very little interaction with de Klerk. I can tell you that the sonar images we are talking about are brand new and have not yet been made public."

"Will they be made public?" Chris asked.

"To some extent, yes," Daniel answered. "It's possible that the resolution of the map around the ship wreck might be reduced a bit so as not to invite too much unwanted attention."

"But Kathryn told me she encouraged the dive boat to bring the divers down there," Chris said. "She clearly wasn't trying to hide the wreck."

"You have to understand the way the dive industry works here in South Africa. Potential spots—wrecks or newly discovered reef features, for instance—are shared sparingly with a few operators, particularly if they are inside any of the marine protected areas. And even then, not all operators are allowed at all the spots."

"So you're saying the captains don't share the locations that are provided to them?" Mac asked.

Daniel nodded. "Exactly. There is no incentive to share. In fact, there is a great deal of incentive to hold the locations a secret."

"But still, the word is going to get out. Someone with a smart phone will note the GPS point where they dive and perhaps share the location and pictures on social media. That happens all the time in the States."

"I see your point, Chris. I do. I'm just telling you how things have worked down here for years."

Donagan turned to Claudia. "Ms. Schwarz is it? I understand that you work in the GIS section at NAMARI. Were you aware of what de Klerk was working on?"

"Yes and no," Claudia answered. "We are a small group responsible for covering the country's entire coastline. So everyone is working on too many projects to pay close attention to what others are doing other than brief summaries at staff meetings." Looking at Daniel she added, "I admit that with such limited resources we end up giving entry-level technicians like de Klerk more responsibility than they should have."

"That is true," Daniel added while shaking his head slowly.

Donagan seemed to study both Daniel and Claudia before he decided to move on. "The men also explained that de Klerk was taken out to Seal Island and fed to the local white sharks, alive."

"Holy crap!" Mac exclaimed. Claudia gasped.

"Yes," Donagan agreed. "Hendrix made the men aware of how unfavorably he viewed that decision."

Hendrix took the opportunity to rejoin the discussion. "Yes, I did. We know that tonight's activity was instigated by man named Jacob Slovo. He is likely not the 'Big Bad' but he is higher up the chain than those two idiots. Slovo is a Namibian with apparent anger issues. He wears a machete on his leg at all times."

"Is Slovo black?" Chris asked. "I think I've seen him; once at the NAMARI building and once at the hospital."

Donagan jumped back into the conversation.

"Yes, you have. The hospital security camera footage confirms that it was Slovo and a man named Pieter Jonker you chased down the stairwell at the hospital."

"Neither of tonight's attackers likes acting on behalf of, as they say, a 'blackie.'" Hendrix was visibly uncomfortable with that term. "It seems that even criminal conspiracies are prone to racism."

"Well if we know who Slovo is, can't we have the police capture him or whoever this Greyling is?" Daniel asked.

"Hold that thought. We'll come back to it," Donagan replied. "Now, Chris, can you tell us the rest of your theory?"

Chris explained his theory about the wreck full of Krugerrands, which was all made much more real for the group when he pulled the single Krugerrand he had found and placed it on the table.

"Mbeke thinks just one of these is worth around $1,500 U.S."

Donagan nodded. "I think that's an accurate estimate."

"We have to tell Kathryn about this," Daniel insisted.

"Perhaps," Chris said, wondering who from inside NAMARI might be leaking information to Greyling and Slovo, including people in the room with him. "But I think we should go out there tomorrow and confirm my theory first."

37

Chris Black yawned as he rolled up to a sitting position. He could feel the swells moving beneath the boat as they steamed out to the wreck site. He was tired, but he'd survive. Mac was still asleep, snoring in the bunk next to him. Though Mac was laboring under major jet lag, Chris had seen Mac sleep through more adverse situations than this so he wasn't particularly worried about him. No one Chris had ever met could catch up on sleep as quickly as Mac Johnson.

The two of them, along with Hendrix and Donagan, had spent much of the night considering the "bigger picture" and planning the next day's operations. Then Hendrix had disappeared again to places unknown with a promise to stay in touch.

Watching Donagan and Hendrix talking quietly before Hendrix had departed, Chris had the feeling that they knew each other previously.

With Mac asleep on the couch, Chris had approached Donagan. "So, Frank—if I may call you Frank—how do you know Hendrix?"

Donagan had looked at Chris briefly, obviously calculating a response, before replying, "Sure, why not. Given what the three of you are planning, and given that I'm now an accomplice, how much more trouble can I get in for telling a few old stories?"

"I guess it depends on the stories."

"Suffice it to say that Hendrix and I have been there and done that."

"And by 'there' you mean?"

"Don't push your luck, Black. We've been to nasty places to do nasty work."

"Got it."

"Hendrix puts on a good show, but he cares. And so does Johnson over there. But then, I suspect you know that."

"You knew Mac already, too?"

"Oh, yeah. I know that you and Johnson have been through some things. Pretty hairy stuff as I've heard tell."

"I guess you could say that. But we've also known each other since elementary school."

"Right. Well, I think that what Johnson went through with Hendrix was also pretty intense.

"I even know how Johnson and Hendrix met. I was *there*."

One of the things that Chris had wondered ever since Mac returned from the military to join him in marine science research was why Hendrix was always available to help whenever Mac seemed to need it. It was clear that they'd been through some action together, but their connection, Chris knew, transcended simple camaraderie.

Even as tired as Chris had been at that point, he'd perked up at this realization. "So you were there. What can you tell me?"

Donagan had paused to look around. Chris guessed that he was confirming whether Mac was actually asleep. "We all found ourselves in a true shithole of a place. Really bad. I was with a group of embassy people being evacuated from what was left of our facility. Hendrix and his team came in on two choppers for the evac. Johnson and his team had only recently rotated into the area of hostilities. They were standing by on a third chopper.

"We were lifting off when the other chopper took a direct RPG hit. It went down fast. That's when everything really went to hell.

"One chopper was down, with many casualties. Ours landed to get as many as we could on board. At that point we were taking heavy fire. The guy next to me took a shot to the neck that killed him instantly.

"We couldn't fit all the wounded on board, so Johnson's chopper came down to assist. We got all the embassy people on the two choppers, and most of the wounded SEALs from Hendrix's team. But Hendrix and two other guys, all three of whom were injured, stayed behind to cover the choppers.

"Johnson was ordered to return with his team and the wounded embassy people, but he jumped out at the last minute to stay behind and help Hendrix."

"Wow."

"Yeah, wow. Fire was now coming in from all angles. All the other SEALS took additional hits, but somehow Johnson was spared. He just kept firing at all comers, emptying a clip, and loading up another.

"By that point a fourth chopper was inbound to evac the remaining SEALs. Johnson kept laying down cover fire as Hendrix and the two others were loaded on the chopper. It was at that moment that Mac was hit in the knee, and then in the chest. His vest took the brunt of the blow to his chest. But as you know, the knee was a different story."

"It sure was. He left the service not long after. The knee still bugs him when we've been in the field for an extended period of time."

"Hendrix didn't, and still doesn't, take what Johnson did lightly."

"I understand. And I don't take what Hendrix has done lightly, either."

Donagan had chuckled at that. "I don't know why Hendrix is so eager to help *you*, but he clearly is."

A rogue swell slammed against the hull, brought Chris out of his reflections, and briefly woke up Mac.

"What?" Mac asked.

"Nothing," Chris said. "That was a wave slapping against the hull. Go back to sleep."

"Everything on schedule?"

"Yes. We alerted Kathryn to my theory about the wreck earlier and to the associated danger. Details regarding last night's attack were left intentionally vague to avoid questions about the whereabouts of the three attackers and to minimize any perceived requirement that Kathryn contact the authorities immediately. Claudia has been sent back to NAMARI under a guard arranged by Kathryn. She should be able to explain more to Kathryn directly. Both Mbeke and Kara have been tasked with work back in NAMARI's main office for the day where they, too, can be protected more reliably."

"So it's just us then?"

"Yep."

"Well, too much of a good thing isn't good, right?" Mac offered before he fell back to sleep.

"I wouldn't know," Chris answered.

Stepping out of the hold onto the back deck, Chris thought more about last night's planning conversation. Donagan had made it clear before he departed around 4:00 a.m. that he was not happy about the role that NAMARI employees were playing in this developing situation. Chris had to admit that it was tough to see an explanation for the way things had recently panned out that didn't involve some NAMARI complicity. How, for instance, had Chris's involvement with this wreck been communicated to Slovo and whomever he is working for? And how did they figure out exactly where he was staying, inside a gated community, with such apparent ease?

Daniel Opperman, despite Donagan's concerns, was up in the wheelhouse driving the boat.

Feeling the boat slow down, Chris stepped back down into the hold and nudged Mac. "Time to get up, sunshine. We're approaching the site."

"Sunshine. Right," a grumpy Mac replied. "I think it's still dinner time *yesterday* for me."

"I can't do much about dinner right now, yesterday or today, but here's an energy bar. Now pull yourself together or I'll have to cut you out of the all the press we'll get when we officially discover the treasure."

"Copy that. Mrs. Johnson didn't raise no suckas, I'm in."

"Well, I think the jury is still out on that point. But let's move beyond it."

As they began to gear up, Mac asked, "Can you remind me who we'll have on deck with me while you and Daniel are in the water?"

"Mbeke really wanted to be out here today, and I wanted him, too. But we just can't expose a grad student to the threat from these guys, whoever they are. So we have two of Hendrix's men."

"Which two?" Mac asked.

"I think one is Roberts and the other is Sanchez, but don't hold me to that. They all kind of fit the same morphotype."

"Good. Sanchez is one mean mofo."

The plan Chris and Mac had devised the previous evening involved both SCUBA divers and the small remotely operated vehicle (ROV) that Chris had asked Mac to bring from California. Chris and Daniel would lead the way on SCUBA, giving them a chance to experience whatever they found in the wreck directly. Mac would pilot the ROV from the surface and follow behind the two divers, recording everything on high-definition video.

The ROV, dubbed the '*Mini-view*' after the much larger *SeaView* ROV that they operated back in Monterey, was to Chris a miracle of modern technology. The robot could dive to two hundred meters, collecting video and still photographs along the way. And it even had a small mechanical manipulator arm for collecting samples. But the real miracle came from the fact that the entire vehicle, along with the control console and the umbilical that connected the ROV to the surface, could fit in three cases small enough to be carried on to a commercial airliner.

Once the boat was tied up at the mooring, and Mac had the ROV control console situated on the back deck, Chris and Daniel entered the water, each wearing full face masks. Unlike their normal SCUBA regulators and masks, which were separate pieces of equipment, the full face mask combined the mask and the regulator into a single unit. The primary advantage of such a system was that Chris and Daniel weren't holding regulators in their mouths; they were free to breathe normally. This allowed them to integrate a communication system into the mask so that they could speak with one another as well as with Mac at the surface. The trick was to learn how to breathe in between sentences.

They quickly descended along the mooring line to the seafloor and then waited for the ROV to catch up. The visibility on the bottom at eighty feet water depth, Chris estimated to be at least thirty feet, much better than on previous dives. So it was quite easy for the divers to spot the ROV headed toward them, its small LED lights illuminating the way.

"Comms check," Chris said. "Daniel, how do you read me?"

"Loud and clear."

"Mac, how do you read me?"

"Loud and clear."

"Good. We have the ROV in sight and will now proceed to wreck number one."

"Copy that," Mac replied.

The first objective of the day's dive was to locate the wreck on which the explosion had occurred. Following their original compass course, and swimming steadily, they found the wreck in under five minutes.

"Whoa," Daniel said in between breaths.

"Yeah." Chris made notations on his dive slate. "Very sad to think of the lives lost only days ago. And it's pretty clear this was no munitions ship. This is a fishing boat."

The now-decimated remnant of the wreck was nestled on a narrow patch of sand in between two high-relief sections of the reef. The wheelhouse was gone, as was much of the bow. Chris could see the spot where he and Kara had located three of the divers' bodies.

"Okay," Chris said. "Mac, have you got some video of this wreck?"

"That's a roger. Ready to move on to wreck number two." Through his neoprene hood Chris could hear the ROV thrusters whirring away as Mac adjusted its position.

"Daniel, I estimate that a course of due south should take us right to the unmapped wreck. Follow me."

"Copy that."

Chris knew this to be the moment of truth; the moment that his theory of the two wrecks would either be confirmed or denied. He was confident that his theory was correct, and that confidence had been bolstered by the fact that no one else, including himself, could come up with a competing theory that fit the facts.

He still was at a loss to explain who, if anyone, from NAMARI had been supplying information to Jacob Slovo and his team. Looking over at Daniel as they swam along the bottom, he was nearly certain it could not be him, even though Hendrix had put Daniel at the top of his suspect list. Daniel was a career scientist with a deep commitment to the protected area in which he worked. Chris just couldn't see how or why Daniel would have gone bad. But as Hendrix had pointed out the night before, "Anyone can be manipulated. We all have our price. Or weaknesses."

Chris also couldn't imagine that either Mbeke or Kara would be involved. That either could be compromised at such an early age seemed unlikely. But again, as Hendrix had pointed out, Chris had only known the two of them for less than a month.

That left Kathryn and Claudia, of the major players at NAMARI that Chris had any contact with, who could be aiding Slovo. Certainly both were in a position to have all the information the bad guys needed. Chris didn't think it was likely, but it was certainly possible. In Claudia's case, he realized he really didn't want it to be her, so he'd have to be careful to keep his emotions in check.

Swimming at what he considered to be "transect speed," meaning the speed at which he would swim his video camera system along a fixed transect when sampling reef fish, Chris and Daniel covered ninety feet in approximately four minutes. The second wreck was just where Chris expected it to be.

He made some additional notes on his slate as they approached the wreck, which clearly had been impacted by the explosion at the other site. A large section of the bow, which had been sealed tight during Chris's earlier visit was now exposed, giving the divers easy access to the contents inside.

Chris checked the dive computer on his wrist. He had started the dive with twenty-eight minutes allowed at this depth, and they had used half of that time so far. That left fourteen minutes before they needed to ascend to a shallower depth.

"Okay. Daniel, I'm reading fourteen minutes remaining on my computer. Let's hang back for a second and let Mac document the wreck's condition. Mac, do you copy that?"

"Loud and clear," Mac replied. "I'll take a trip around the wreck and then focus on the exposed section of the bow. You boys stand by."

"Actually Mac, I think we'll follow the ROV around to see if we can see any evidence of tampering. We still don't know what caused the other wreck to explode. If the bad guys wired it, they may have done the same here."

A lap around the wreck revealed no evidence of any type of tampering. After Mac collected a couple of minutes of video around the opening at the bow, he backed off the ROV. Chris and Daniel then moved in.

On many occasions Chris had explained to students that the penetration of a submerged wreck can be either extremely dangerous, or no problem at all. He had experienced both conditions over the years, and he knew that one of the biggest concerns when entering deep into a wreck included getting disoriented and subsequently lost or trapped inside. It was shocking how easily a diver could get mixed up once inside a wreck. Poor diver buoyancy could lead them to kick up fine sediment that had accumulated over decades instantly reducing the visibility within the wreck to zero. Once that happened, finding one's way out of the wreck became difficult at best.

Chris knew the wreck diving community had a variety of approaches to reducing risk on complicated wreck dives, including intricate networks of lines strung throughout the wreck. He'd experienced something similar while diving at the *Poseidon* Undersea Laboratory in the Florida Keys, where, because of the issues associated with saturation diving, divers were effectively cave diving. At *Poseidon,* as well as in caves, lines were put out with small plastic arrows attached to the line at regular intervals so that if you got lost and couldn't see anything, at least the arrows would lead you in the right direction.

But in the case of the wreck before them, with a single large opening leading into a single interior space, much of the risk was already reduced. The divers swam through the opening in single file, being careful not to snag their SCUBA gear on the ragged edges of the opening.

Once into the hold, both divers paused to check their buoyancy and to take in what was in front of them. Sitting on the seafloor at eighty feet water depth, the wreck was still bathed in sunlight. However, little of that light penetrated into the hull, so Chris slowly panned his powerful dive light across the gap in the outer hull he'd found during the previous dive. He counted eighteen barrels, five more than he'd originally estimated from the look inside the hold on the previous dive.

"Mac, do you copy?"

"Loud and clear. What is the status inside?"

"I count eighteen barrels." He tried to move one of the barrels and quickly realized that that was not going to be possible without major assistance. "They aren't going to be moved without sizeable lift bags."

"Copy," Mac said. "Anything else in there?"

"Standby," Chris replied, as he continued to pan his light around the hold. Something white flashed within the beam and he slowly swam over to investigate.

"Daniel, come over here and look at this."

Daniel replied, "What did you . . . Oh, man."

There were two human skulls lying amidst a pile of bones resting on the sediment that had accumulated over the years the wreck had been on the seafloor. The jaw bone of one skull had separated, but the other remained attached and slightly agape. There was a noticeable hole in the left side of the skull just behind the temple.

"Mac, we have the remains of at least two humans down here. One of the skulls has what looks like a bullet hole. You'd better get this on video. We'll back out of here slowly so you can fly the ROV in."

"Copy that."

"But let me check something first." Monitoring his allowable bottom time closely, Chris reached down to the sheath on his thigh and extracted his flat-nosed dive knife as he approached one of the barrels. He then used the flat end of the knife to pry open the top of the barrel. Assuming that the wreck had been down since the Apartheid days more than thirty years earlier, Chris was surprised to see the lid come off the barrel so easily.

Both divers audibly gasped when Daniel shined his dive light into the barrel. The light reflected off hundreds of shiny gold Krugerrands visible at the top of the barrel, each looking as though it had just been minted.

"We're going to need a bigger boat," Chris said, quoting *Jaws*, one of his favorite movies.

"What?" Daniel asked.

"Nothing. That's a lot of gold."

"Yes. I think we're going to have to tell someone about this."

Chris couldn't help but smile at Daniel's understatement, and he immediately began considering their options.

38

Chris, Mac, and Hendrix watched the sun set over the horizon west of Kometjie from the rooftop deck of Chris's granny flat. The mood was subdued. Chris assumed that, like him, the others were trying to wrap their minds around what they had found today. That plus the fact that at least fourteen people had already died because of the treasure, and no one knew exactly what the threat level was moving forward.

"I understand why you came down here Black," Hendrix said in between sips of his Carling Black Label. "It's beautiful, and it's far from Carmel. But eventually you'll need to get back into the game. You can't stay down here forever."

"I think the game came to him," Mac said.

"That's true," Hendrix replied, looking at Chris. "You find trouble at least as easily as I do. But let's face it, we know I'm *looking* for it."

The thrill of the discovery had worn off over the afternoon as the feverish planning had set in. Chris looked out over the horizon and realized that maybe six months were not going to be necessary to replenish his reserves. He was nowhere near replenished, but he was nonetheless ready to go home to Carmel—to sit on the white sand of the main beach on evenings just like this, with Thig panting at his side, and take it all in. It had been too long since they'd done a fire in one of the fire pits with his students, too long since he'd been able to sit back and enjoy their ceaseless banter.

Undaunted by Chris's silence, Hendrix continued, "Well, I know you scientists are fond of data, so I'll put it to you this way: I think the data pretty strongly suggest that you, too, are looking for it." Then Hendrix sat back in his chair looking, Chris thought, rather pleased with his penetrating insights.

The three sat comfortably watching the sun set when the ambiance was broken by Hendrix's cell phone ringing. He brought the phone up to his ear and said, "Go."

He listened, nodded his head two or three times, and then said before hanging up, "Copy that. Stand by."

"Everything go according to plan?" Mac asked.

Hendrix reached for another beer. "So far. But as I've heard Black say on more than one occasion, 'the day is young.'"

The "plan," such as it was, was complicated and imperfect, Chris thought. But it was the best they could come up with given the many variables they faced, prominent among those being the fact that outside of the three of them, and possibly Donagan, they did not know who to trust. He rubbed his hand over the scar on his chest; it was no longer hurting every day, and had now moved on to the itchy phase.

Chris's smartphone, which was sitting on the table between them, vibrated from an incoming text message. He leaned over to read the text without touching the phone.

"Uh, oh," Chris said with a tone that made both Mac and Hendrix sit up in their chairs. "Daniel says he just got back to the NAMARI office. Neither Kathryn nor Claudia reported in for work today. And there's no sign of the guards that were supposed to be keeping an eye on them."

"What happened?" Mac asked.

"Hang on, let me text him back." Chris asked for clarification and for any word on Mbeke and Kara.

The reply came almost instantly. "Mbeke and Kara OK. Nothing from Kathryn or Claudia via phone, email, or text."

Here's where the "plan" falls apart, Chris thought, his mind immediately focusing on the potential danger to Claudia. If she was in trouble, it was because of her association with him.

Hendrix hopped up from his chair, grabbed his phone, and moved over to the other side of the deck to make a call.

"Okay, we've kept Daniel in the dark with respect to key aspects of the plan, just in case he is the problem," Mac said to Chris. "I have to ask again, do we really trust him?"

Chris stared at the text message. "I don't like keeping him in the dark. I honestly don't know who we can trust. But if we can trust anyone I've met down here, Daniel would be the guy. I just don't see him willingly helping these guys. Let me try Claudia's phone."

She picked up immediately. "Chris."

"Claudia where—"

"Dr. Black," a new, much more menacing voice said. "So nice to hear your voice."

"Who is this?" Chris asked, looking at Mac, who was in turn signaling Hendrix.

"I think you know who this is."

"Slovo."

"That's right. So you know my name. I'm sorry we didn't get to meet at the hospital."

"Or at NAMARI," added Chris, his mind reviewing what he remembered of Slovo. "What do you want?"

"Nothing. Absolutely nothing."

"Then why are we talking?"

"I wanted to talk to you just once before I carve up this pretty young thing, so that when you find the pieces spread out along the coast you will know that it's your fault."

39

Mac and Hendrix moved in closer to listen.

"That's right, Black. I'm going to kill your little friend here, kill her boss, and walk away with the gold, too. I may have to have some fun with your friend first. You can mention that to your paramilitary friends, too."

Chris took a deep breath. "Slovo, this is just a job for you. You're working for someone, right? Someone named Greyling?"

"Why?"

"Just tell me."

"I have partners in this operation, yes."

"Okay, then before you touch either one of our colleagues, before you even look at them harshly, I recommend that you or one of your partners sail out to the wreck and take quick look around."

There was a long pause on the other end of the phone.

"Go look, Slovo. Then call me back. And remember, do not touch our colleagues. Do you have that, Slovo?"

"I'm going to kill you, Black."

"We'll see, Slovo. We'll see. Have one of your partners call me at this number. I'll be waiting."

Deep into the planning meeting the night before, Hendrix had stepped away to "contact a colleague." Chris had never met anyone with colleagues as widespread as Hendrix. Hendrix either knew someone, or he knew someone who knew someone, no matter where he was on the planet. In the present situation, the question had been what to do with the gold if they did find it. Chris had read entire books dedicated the convoluted legal processes associated with the recovery of treasure from the seafloor. In some cases, court decisions about ownership took years, bankrupting the team who discovered the treasure in the first place. In others, the ownership was awarded quickly, but then the logistics of recovery ended up taking years, often with the same effect.

It was also clear to both Chris and Donagan that not all was right with NAMARI. Whoever was behind this evidently had a long reach and was getting information from someone behind the scenes. So, while no one in the room had any interest in the treasure, all were in agreement that it should be kept out of the hands of the bad guys. And since the interrogation of the two attackers had also yielded the realization that the perpetrators' recovery efforts were forthcoming, they couldn't wait for the slow wheels of justice to turn. They had to act, and that essentially meant stealing the treasure first. Hendrix insisted on a different interpretation; something he called "preemptive assistance" in recovering the treasure.

The colleague Hendrix contacted was a marine salvage expert and a former British commando by the name of Samantha White. Her eighty-foot-long salvage vessel, cheekily named the *Queen of England*, was already in False Bay for a different job. The eighteen barrels that Chris and Daniel counted in the hull of the wreck posed no big challenge for Samantha and her team. They could recover the barrels to the ship by the end of the day and then retreat offshore until they received guidance from Hendrix as to the next step.

"So just to clarify," Mac had said as Chris and Daniel broke down their SCUBA gear earlier that day, "We've turned over a sizeable treasure lying in South African waters to a British-registered salvage operation whose first act will be to take said treasure and depart South African waters? That's our plan?"

"Why are you re-stating a plan in which you played a non-trivial role in forming?" Chris asked with some exasperation. "How does that help us?"

"I just want to understand, for the record, which decision it was that finally landed us in a foreign penal system. Lord knows we've deserved it before now."

"Oh, I think Donagan, whoever he really is, is going to be able to keep *me* out of prison. But you? I'm not so sure. I'll send you a copy of *The Count of Monte Cristo* to pass the time in your cell."

Daniel had been horrified by the plan. "Chris, you cannot remove anything from that wreck! It is South African property. It belongs to us, and we need to alert the proper authorities immediately. I can't believe you are even considering this! What are you thinking?

"Kathryn is going to be furious. And rightly so. I've never heard of something so brash as this. It is really unbelievable."

Chris had made eye contact with Mac but let Daniel vent his frustrations. Eventually, he'd told Chris he could not support the plan, but he would also not do anything to jeopardize it. They'd parted company after arriving at the dock with Chris fairly certain he'd compromised the close friendship that had brought him to South Africa in the first place.

40

"He picked a good spot," Frank Donagan said, "Chapman's Peak Drive. You've got a steep cliff going up the hill on one side and a steep cliff down to the ocean on the other."

Willem Greyling had called Chris's cell phone two hours prior, right at sunset. Twenty-four hours after Chris had spoken to Slovo, and shortly after Greyling's men had returned from the wreck site with the harsh realization that the treasure was being removed from the wreck by a salvage company.

"You have no idea who you're fucking with my little friend," Greyling had said. "No idea."

"You realize Apartheid is over, right? You and your pals are just a nasty asterisk on South African history," Chris had noted.

"Yes, things have changed. I'll grant you that. But if you think we can't get to you, you're wrong. I have a network vaster than you could ever imagine. We are everywhere, I assure you."

"Well, everywhere except out recovering your gold. Now, let me speak to Claudia and Kathryn."

"They're not available."

"Then neither is your gold. Available, that is."

"I WANT MY FUCKING MONEY!"

"I couldn't care less about your gold or your desire for it. I want to speak to the two women. *Now.*"

Chris could hear shuffling on the other end, and a door open. Greyling said something in Afrikaner and then suddenly Claudia was on the phone.

"Chris, it's me."

"Claudia, are you hurt?"

"No, we're fine."

"Is Kathryn there with you?"

"Yes, I'm here," Kathryn said from the background. "Chris, removing the treasure from the wreck is a violation of both South African and international maritime law. What were you thinking?"

"Kathryn, let's stay focused on getting you and Claudia back safely, then we can worry about my future. Claudia, do you remember the conversation we had a couple of days ago?"

"Yes, I do."

"Good. I—"

"That is quite enough," Greyling said, grabbing the phone from Claudia. "Lookout Point. 1300 hours, tomorrow. Come alone. No law enforcement. I know that you cannot bring the gold with you, but I want some type of assurance that you will lead me to it."

"What type of assurance?" Chris had asked.

"You'll figure something out," Greyling said, and then closed the line.

Hendrix, Mac, and Chris had been planning since the call ended. Donagan had only just arrived.

"Okay. Donagan's here," Chris said. "Before we do anything further, I want to know who Greyling is."

As if on cue, Donagan reached into the weathered leather bag he'd brought and extracted a file folder that looked to Chris as though it was two inches thick.

"This is the *smaller* of the two files the embassy has on Willem Greyling," Donagan explained. "Think of it as an executive summary."

Hendrix took the file from Donagan and began to look through it, while Donagan continued to explain, "He had a number of different positions during the Apartheid era. The early years appear to have been fairly innocuous, different low-level administrative positions."

"It says here he was the Director of Internal Security," Hendrix said. "That sounds vague."

"Right. Around 1978 Greyling was elevated to the position Hendrix is talking about. There isn't anything in the file that explains the rather rapid ascent to a director position. But he occupied that position until the Apartheid government collapsed in the early nineties."

Pointing at the file, Donagan continued, "The file does include, however, a long list of actions Greyling took while in that position."

"What kind of actions?" Mac asked.

"It says here that in 1982 Greyling was responsible for an entire village being essentially eradicated," Hendrix quoted what he'd read. "It looks like six teenagers from the village were arrested in Cape Town while advocating for the overthrow of the government. Greyling chose to make an example of the six teens, and when the villagers responded negatively, he used force—excessive force."

"What's he been doing since Apartheid ended?" Chris asked.

"I asked a colleague just that question," Donagan replied. "She said that he'd 'pulled a Hoover,' which I took to mean that he'd accumulated so much information on so many people during his days in office, he was simply too dangerous to mess with."

"So he may have been wreaking havoc all along?" Mac asked.

"He could have been doing a number of things," Hendrix said. "There are pages and pages here of documented actions against people he characterized as his 'opponents.' This guy literally knows where all the bodies are buried."

Mac shook his head. "If I weren't so appalled, I might be impressed. But what do we do about him?"

No one said anything.

Finally Chris stood up. "Is this one demented old bastard more capable then the group we have sitting here in this room? I don't think so. We go get him, and we get Claudia and Kathryn back."

"He will have thought several steps ahead," Donagan said. "He'll have a plan."

"Yes, it's not a bad spot he's picked," Hendrix concurred. "Not great if you're worried about law enforcement. They could easily block the road in both directions. But they're counting on our not contacting the authorities. And given that we are now international criminals, I guess we won't be."

"There is no easy access to the ocean along this stretch of coast, and the overland route is a non-starter," Mac said. "And there's no place to land a chopper, either. They're clearly not planning to get out of there quickly."

Donagan looked at Chris. "It will be challenging to cover you given that we don't know where they will take you, and it's very likely they have no intention of letting you or the ladies out of there alive."

"I agree," Hendrix said. "I know you care about Claudia and Kathryn, but neither is likely to survive. Sending you in is only going to add you to the list."

"But you're going anyway," Mac said, knowing the answer.

"Yes, I am," Chris said.

"Alright, then here's what I suggest," Hendrix said.

41

The air temperature was a pleasant seventy-eight degrees as Chris Black drove from his rental house in Kommetjie through Noordhoek and onto the Chapman's Peak Drive, which wound along the cliffs above the Atlantic side of the Cape of Good Hope. This was his third time through this area since arriving in South Africa, and to Chris it was uncanny how similar this road was to the stretch of California's Highway 1 just south of Carmel. Both had sheer rock faces dotted with patches of vegetation, dropping precipitously into the churning surf below. Both had roads that clung to the rock face to the best of their ability. And given the number of times he had cheated death on Highway 1, the irony was not lost on him that he was now planning to do the same thing here on Chapman's Peak Drive.

As the road climbed up out of Noordhoek, the traffic was lighter than Chris expected. A beautiful day like this one should bring out the tourists in droves. He glanced down to his left and believed he could see the *Queen of England* steaming into view. Right on time, he thought.

The road peaked briefly and the parking lot for the lookout point opened up to his left. There was a smattering of people mulling around, along with three cars and a small white van. He pulled off the road and parked next to the van. Jacob Slovo was sitting in the driver seat with the window rolled down.

Chris marveled at the incongruity of the scene; tourists innocently taking in a beautiful vista, blissfully unaware that a killer like Slovo was in their midst. How many times per day did average citizens come into such close proximity with homicidal maniacs, Chris wondered, before concluding that it was probably more frequent than anyone would want to admit.

He took a single deep breath to calm himself and rolled down the passenger side window of his SUV.

"Get in the back," Slovo said.

"Where are my colleagues?"

"Not here. How stupid do you think we are, Black? I'm sure you've got your group of soldier friends all over this hillside, waiting to 'take us out,' as you Yanks say. Now get in the back of the van."

Getting into any vehicle with a man like Slovo was not high on Chris's list of things to do for the day, and a windowless van didn't make it any easier. But this was not unanticipated, either. He rolled up the window and got out of his car.

A man stepped from behind Slovo's van and motioned for Chris to lift up his arms so he could be frisked. While that happened, Chris briefly surveilled the hillside and wondered if Hendrix and Donagan had anyone out there under cover, indeed.

Once frisked, and under gunpoint, Chris opened the sliding door of the van and instantly regretted it. The interior of the van reeked of death, and he hoped, more than he cared to admit to himself, that Claudia was not under the grey tarp visible on the far side of the van's interior. He'd been able to keep his feelings for Claudia at an arm's length during the events of the last two days, but he realized that it was going to be nearly impossible now that he was coming into direct contact with Slovo.

"What's under that tarp?" Chris asked. As the van door was being closed, Chris noticed that Slovo was wearing his seat belt.

"Don't worry," Slovo said. "It's just the three dead guards you paid to watch the two women. We won't kill the women until you're there to enjoy it. Now sit down and shut the fuck up."

Chris did not want Slovo to get too comfortable with this power dynamic. If they were all going to survive this day, it would be important to have the bad guys unbalanced, unsure as to their likely success. So, as he feigned sitting down, and gambling that, to Slovo's boss, he was more important alive than dead, Chris reached out and jabbed Slovo hard in the face with his right hand. Slovo's head whipped sideways and hit the driver's side door frame with a heavy thud.

"Fuck *you*, Slovo. If anyone's going to die today, it'll be you."

Slovo took several seconds to recover from the blow. Chris watched Slovo's reaction in the rear-view mirror as the immediate pain and shock began to wear off. There was anger in his eyes now but also Chris was sure he saw some hesitancy as well. Maybe this strategy was paying off.

"See, Slovo? Why don't you wave to my friend over there before he shoots you," Chris said, pointing out the front windshield toward the bushes beyond the guard rail.

As Slovo instinctively turned to look at the friend who was not there, Chris reached out and hit him again, this time with an open palm to the back of his head. Slovo was propelled forward and hit his forehead on the steering wheel.

The howl that came from Slovo next seemed to Chris to reflect shock, pain, fear, and rage simultaneously. Trapped by his seatbelt in the front seat, with his machete strapped to his right leg against the driver's side door, Slovo's options for retaliation were limited. He was going to have to get out of the van, and get Chris out of the van as well, before the machete could be brought into play.

Just then the handheld radio sitting on the dashboard crackled, "What are you doing, Slovo? Get Black down here now! Copy?"

Slovo grabbed the steering wheel and violently rocked forward and backward, shaking the entire van in the process. But then he calmed down sufficiently to turn the key in the ignition. Chris held on to one of the internal rails in the van as Slovo slammed it into reverse and then pulled out onto the road.

As they rocketed down the curvy road, Chris noted the landmarks he'd memorized pass by. They passed the hiking trail on the right and the café he'd never been to. Then, after barely negotiating a left turn, Slovo pulled the van off the road and into what Mac had dubbed "lookout #2."

The van came to a halting stop. Chris watched Slovo for any movement, but the rear door of the van was opened behind him and there stood an old man. Chris assumed it was Greyling. He was dressed in an old tweed coat, with a black vest beneath it. The wind coming up the cliffs from the ocean blew several long white strands of Greyling's comb-over hairdo.

As he tried to control his errant hair, Greyling said, "Please come out of the van, Dr. Black. It is time for us to discuss our deal."

Stepping out of the van, Chris was looking around for any sign of Claudia and Kathryn when someone hit him hard on the back of his neck, knocking him down to his hands and knees. He cringed at the pain and blinked away the stars spiraling around in his peripheral vision.

"Pick him up," Greyling said, and two men grabbed Chris's arms and lifted him to a standing position.

"Now, Dr. Black. I'm sure that Slovo would like to slice you up with his big knife. To be honest, I don't know who he hates more, you or me. But that is no matter. I want my gold."

Chris noted that there were no weapons visible and the two men holding him up were doing so in a way that wouldn't necessarily be seen as hostile from a casual passerby on the road.

"Where are my colleagues?"

Greyling motioned over his shoulder. An identical van to the one Chris had just exited backed up to the group. A third man materialized from behind Chris and opened the rear doors of the van. Claudia and Kathryn were sitting on benches opposite one another. Their hands were zip-tied in front of them and they were both gagged, but neither seemed otherwise harmed. Defiance was clear in their eyes.

"You see? They are fine. Now where is my gold?"

"Let me speak to them first," Chris said. For that he was hit behind his knees. He would have fallen again had the two men not been holding him up.

"Let me assure you, Dr. Black, you're not in a position to give any orders or make requests. I will ask you one more time and then I'll let Slovo begin to cut off pieces of you very slowly. Where is my gold?"

Chris wondered at the wisdom of their grand plan. It all seemed to make sense when they were safely ensconced in his rental flat looking over a map. But the reality of standing here on a roadside turn out being beat on by hired thugs was something else altogether.

Chris motioned with his head over Greyling's left shoulder. There, visible through the trees, was the *Queen of England* sitting just offshore.

"All of it is on that ship?" Greyling's old, watery eyes gleamed.

"All eighteen barrels full of Krugerrands, minus the one coin I have in my front pocket. What do we do now?"

"Now? Now I let Slovo carve you up, then kill the two women. Then my colleagues in the Coast Guard will go out to seize that ship and arrest everyone on board. We don't know where your paramilitary friends are at the moment, but we'll find them soon enough."

Chris could feel a sharp object, which he assumed was Slovo's machete, poking into his back and breaking the skin.

"You see, Dr. Black? You have failed to do anything other than to momentarily impede our efforts. In fact, by violating the law and extracting the gold for us you have actually been of great assistance. It would have been much more cumbersome for us to recover the gold ourselves. So I thank you."

Greyling turned to the man at Chris's right. "Kill them all, starting with Black. But do it in the vans. Go!"

Chris made eye contact with Claudia; at the rate things were going, possibly for the last time. Then, while anticipating a strike from the machete at any second, he quickly relaxed in the arms of the two men, forcing them to struggle to keep his sagging body off the ground.

On cue, high powered rifle shots struck the men on either side of Chris, killing them instantly. As he fell to the ground, he could hear several other shots hitting men and vehicles around him. Chris quickly leapt up to a crouching position and looked for Slovo and Greyling. Greyling had been hit in the upper torso and shoulder and was lying on the pavement moaning. Two other men were down behind Chris, but there was no sign of Slovo.

With the gunfire dropping off, Chris stood up and approached Greyling. He kneeled down to extract a revolver from a holster under Greyling's jacket and then tossed it out of reach.

Chris. "Ouch. That looks like it hurts, my little friend," Chris said as he patted Greyling's damaged shoulder. "I'm sure someone will be along shortly to take care of you."

". . . going to kill you." Greyling replied weakly.

"You just keep telling yourself that. My mom tells me a positive attitude is critical for successful recovery." Chris stood up.

As he started toward the van holding Claudia and Kathryn, watching in what felt like slow motion, Chris saw Slovo come from nowhere and jump into the driver's seat of the van, which had been idling in place. Slovo hit the accelerator and the van lurched out onto the road. The lurch sent Kathryn rolling out the back of the van onto the pavement.

Chris looked up at Claudia as the van doors swung open briefly, before swinging back and closing. Slovo raced off down the road heading north.

Chris ran over to Kathryn and checked her for injuries. "Kathryn, are you okay?" he asked as he removed the gag from her mouth.

"I'm okay, I'm okay. But what about Claudia?"

"She's still in the van with Slovo."

While he was talking to Kathryn, Chris saw an old, red mini-van that had been parked further down in the parking lot accelerate out of its spot and head right toward him. It skidded to a stop next to him. Mac was behind the wheel.

"I can't drive on the left side, get in!" Mac moved over to the passenger seat.

"I'm coming, too!" Kathryn said before Chris could discourage her. He ran around the driver's side door and got in. There was no sign of Slovo's van on the road, so he punched the accelerator.

42

"The point is this, we never stop searching, Chris. We never stop. Do you understand?"

"I think so, Dad," an eight-year-old Chris Black answered his father. "It's like, Luke and Leia never gave up on finding Han Solo. They tracked him all the way to Tatooine and rescued him from Jabba the Hut. They could have given up and left him in the carbonite."

"That's right." Andrew Black had smiled at his young son's use of a *Star Wars* story line to relate to his Vietnam-era wisdom. "I'm here today with you because my friends didn't give up on me. Just like Luke Skywalker, they kept searching until they found me."

"They found you in the jungle, right?"

"Yep. They sure did. I was hurt and very sick. But they found me, and they brought me home to you and mom."

"Pretty cool."

"It *was* pretty cool."

"Can I go back in the water now dad?"

"Of course, Chris. Get back in the water. I'll join you in a couple of minutes."

"What'd you say?" Mac slipped a knife from a side pocket on his pants and cut the zip ties off Kathryn's hands.

"We never give up," Chris replied, his eyes not deviating from the road in front of him.

"Thank you, whoever you are," Kathryn said. "Chris, who is this person? Who shot those men back there? What the hell is going on?"

Chris was driving fast. "Kathryn, Claudia is still tied up in that van with a very bad guy, who's working for even worse guys. We have to catch them before he hurts her, or worse. Can we focus on that right now?"

Kathryn inhaled deeply. "Of course. But can I ask this person who he is?"

Mac turned around in his front seat and introduced himself. "Hi, I'm Mac Johnson. I work with Chris back in California."

"Are you some kind of policeman or government agency employee?"

"No, ma'am. I'm an ROV pilot and general all-around handy man."

"An ROV pilot?" Kathryn swallowed hard. "Okay. Thank you. Proceed."

"Mac, if I recall correctly the road is going to straighten out sometime soon. Where could he be going?"

Mac pulled out his smart phone and started mapping their path. "Up ahead looks like Hout Bay. From there he can either continue north on a coastal road very similar to this called Victoria Road, or he can veer to the right on any number of roads and enter Cape Town proper. I can't see him continuing on coast road, not enough options."

"Agreed," Chris said, as the road straightened out. The white van was not visible down the road for several miles. "And that means we've lost them. I'm not looking at the map, but basically they can go anywhere into Cape Town, correct?"

"That's correct," Mac said. "I think we should alert Hendrix to see what he can come up with."

"I concur," Chris said, but he was not feeling hopeful.

"There is a third option," Kathryn said from the backseat.

Catching her eye in the rearview mirror, Chris said, "Tell me."

"While we were being held by this Willem Greyling person, I overhead both Greyling and two of his, his, henchmen I guess you'd call them, talking about Jacob Slovo. Apparently Slovo is a former river boat captain from Namibia. So isn't it possible that a person like that might try the water instead of a road?"

Chris looked at Mac. "What does it look like in Hout Bay?"

While Mac fiddled with his smartphone, Kathryn said, "There's a small marina on the western shore of Hout Bay. He might be able to find a boat there."

"Got it." Mac looked down at his phone. "You're going to want to slow down up ahead was we approach town, but we should only be five minutes away."

"Remember, I live here," Kathryn said. "I'll direct you in. May I please borrow your phone Mr. Johnson?"

Mac handed her his phone, and both he and Chris listened from the front seat as she contacted a marine mammal rescue center in the Hout Bay marina where NAMARI kept a twenty-four-foot Boston Whaler tied up at the dock. Someone at the center was told to get the Whaler ready for them.

"Just in case," Kathryn said while handing Mac his phone.

Chris's concern that they would not be able to tell if Slovo had tried for a vessel at the marina was nullified as soon as they approached the entrance. The white van was parked diagonally across a small chain fence bordering the wharf parking lots, both the driver's side door and the rear doors were ajar. There was a crowd of onlookers standing around the van. More than one person was pointing down the wharf.

"Kathryn, where is this marine mammal center?"

"Keep driving, Chris. It's up here on the left. There! Turn in where that grey car just pulled out."

Within minutes they were on the dock. Kathryn talked to the center employees, while Mac prepped the boat for departure.

"I see them!" Chris pointed to a small cabin cruiser speeding out of the harbor in a no wake zone. Slovo was at the wheel.

"We've got two outboard motors, but that boat is a lot faster than this one," Mac said.

"We've got to try. Let's go."

Kathryn elected to remain behind and contact the authorities, while Chris and Mac jumped into the Whaler.

Mac expertly guided the Whaler out of the slip in which it was tied up, around the floating dock in front of it, and out of the harbor entrance.

"Do you have your bag of tricks with you?" Chris asked, interested in anything he could use as a weapon as he watched Slovo speed away.

"Nope. It's back at the lookout. I had to get going too quickly." Reaching into his belt he pulled out a pistol Hendrix had tossed to him. "We've got this."

Mac wound the Whaler's engines up as the boat reached twenty-five knots. Rounding the point to the west of the marina, they left the relative protection of the bay and entered the open Atlantic Ocean. Chris knew that once out of the protective embayment, the swells would pick up significantly. At the speed they were travelling, every swell, even every ripple in the water, shook the boat violently as it passed. Chris stood behind Mac, his legs spread wide and both hands gripping the back of the seat firmly. Spray came over the bow with each passing swell, drenching both Mac and Chris.

"There's a swell running out here," Mac yelled over the engine noise. "It's going to get dicey. Hang on."

As the size of the waves increased, Slovo's boat was only visible to Chris when Mac crested the peaks of the larger swells. He looked down to see the water level in the boat reach his ankles.

"We can't keep up this speed in these swells," Mac yelled. "I'm going to have to slow down."

Chris knew that Boston Whalers were highly sought after for their stability, but he judged the swells to be at least eight feet from crest to trough. These were not waters they wanted to navigate in such a small boat. He knew the cabin cruiser would also be slowing down, but it was much better suited to open ocean conditions than the Whaler was. The danger was heightened because Slovo was fleeing northward parallel to shore. That meant incoming swells were hitting the vessels from the side, which dramatically increased the probability of capsizing.

"Incoming!"

Chris instinctively knew what Mac was talking about and braced himself for impact. The swell hit them on the port side as Mac turned the boat into the seas. Chris's feet were lifted off the deck two feet, but he was able to maintain his grip on the seat. Mac somehow held tight to the helm.

"We can't take too many more like that."

"Look!" Chris pointed at the cabin cruiser that had slowed to a stop and was now bouncing precariously on the swells. He could see Slovo climb down a ladder from the cockpit, his machete drawn. Claudia emerged from a cabin and stepped onto the back deck, carrying what looked to Chris like a flare gun. Chris's pulse quickened as he considered the danger Claudia was now in. The cabin cruiser disappeared behind a swell. Rising again into view seconds later, the entire back deck was illuminated by a brilliant orange glow.

43

"We have to get over there!" yelled Chris over the combined roar of the waves and the hum of the Whaler's two outboard motors. He kept his eyes fixed on the cabin cruiser. He could see neither Claudia nor Slovo.

Struggling to keep the small boat upright in the turbulent waters, Mac responded with equivalent volume, "Working on it."

Now drifting with the swell, the cabin cruiser was being pushed shoreward, where rocks awaited the crashing waves. Chris hadn't been able to make out Claudia or Slovo and feared the worst.

It took less than five minutes for Mac to close the distance to the drifting vessel. "This is going to be tight," he said. "If you move up to the bow, I'll bring the Whaler in to the stern of the boat. You'll need to jump across, and we'll need to time it perfectly with the swell."

"Will you try to tie up?"

"No. We're drifting too close to those breaking waves along the shore. You should get over there, figure out what's going on, and get out."

"Let's do it," Chris said.

Mac watched the swells carefully, which were now coming in ten second intervals. When the boat drifted into the trough, Mac expertly brought the Whaler up alongside and Chris jumped onto the cabin cruiser's stern gunwale. From there he dropped down onto the back deck.

Claudia was alive. She was sitting against the starboard gunwale holding her hands over her side. Blood was leaking out through her fingers.

"I'm here, Claudia."

"I'm not feeling so great."

"Where's Slovo?"

"Here," came an ominous reply from behind Chris. He turned to see Slovo coming out of the cabin. He was favoring his left shoulder, where his shirt had disintegrated and his skin was bubbling with what Chris estimated to be third degree burns. Slovo's machete was in his right hand.

Without taking his eyes off Slovo, Chris reached down and grabbed a towel lying on the deck. He wrapped it around his right forearm.

Pointing towards the shore, Chris offered, "Slovo, the boat's headed for the rocks. What do you say we postpone killing each other until we get to safety?"

Slovo sneered. "I don't think so Black. We finish this here."

"Suit yourself!" Chris yelled over the waves. He stepped in front of Claudia to put himself between her and Slovo, keeping his eyes on the machete. His feet were spaced apart widely in an attempt to remain stable despite the violent rocking of the boat.

Taking stock of the situation, Chris could see only two factors in his favor: Slovo's damaged left shoulder and the deteriorating ocean conditions, which Chris calculated would benefit him more, given is extensive experience at sea.

When the attack came, it was vicious and lightning quick. But it was also awkward and off target as a large wave crashed over the stern. Chris was able to fend off Slovo's initial swing of the machete with the towel on his forearm. Grabbing ahold of the aluminum ladder with his left hand to stabilize himself, Chris struck out with a close-quarters kick to Slovo's damaged left shoulder, connecting partially with the wounded area.

Slovo screamed in pain as another large wave rocked the boat, separating the two men briefly and turning the boat sideways to the oncoming swells. Knowing that the next wave might flip the boat, Chris wagered that a capsized boat in this surf would be a bigger danger than Slovo and his machete. He climbed the short ladder up to the boat's cockpit, looking back to confirm that Slovo was not right on top of him.

The upper deck of the boat was enclosed by canvas on three sides, with the front windshield the only permanent structure. Plastic windows were sewn into the canvas facing aft. Chris grabbed for the helm, trying to turn the bow into the oncoming waves before the next one hit, knowing that a bow-on angle was the safest route for the vessel through the surf.

The bow had almost come around when it was launched up into the air by an eight-foot wall of white water. Chris lost his grip on the helm, falling backwards against the canvas enclosure. He could feel several of the metal clasps that held the canvas in place snap and detach under his weight.

To his right, Chris could see Slovo struggling to climb the ladder while keeping his machete in his hand. He scanned the rest of the cockpit, looking for anything that might serve as a weapon and chastising himself for not grabbing the pistol from Mac when he'd had the chance. Finding no suitable weapon, and seeing another wave coming their way, Chris regained control of the helm and brought the bow straight into it.

The wave hit just as Slovo reached the top of the ladder. Slovo struck out with the machete, but Chris was able to dodge to his left and avoid it. With nothing to hold onto, Slovo fell backwards toward the opening in the canvas, but was able to stabilize himself. His eyes flaring, Slovo attacked again, this time less awkwardly, and Chris took the full brunt of the machete on his forearm, blood instantly staining the towel from a wound underneath.

Chris could see Slovo winding up for another attack and realized that he would not be able to weather another impact to his already damaged arm. As the boat dropped into a trough before an oncoming wave, Slovo lost his balance in the midst of his attack. Chris took the opportunity to push off the deck and launch himself at Slovo's upper body. His momentum, aided by the rocking boat, sent both men hurtling toward the stern.

Under Slovo's full weight, the canvas enclosure tore completely free and Slovo fell to the deck below. The impact with Slovo's body had slowed Chris's momentum enough to give him time to grab hold of the canvas, which was now flapping in the wind, and keep himself from falling.

As the boat rocked with the next swell, Chris swung out into space, clinging tightly to the canvas flap. Momentarily hanging out over the water, Chris feared he was going to be tossed off the boat. Looking up, he could see that the canvas flap he clung onto was tearing free from the rest of the enclosure. Falling quickly as the canvas tore, Chris was seconds away from dropping into the sea when the deck appeared again below his feet. Releasing his grip, he landed awkwardly, but upright on the back deck.

"Chris!" Claudia was lying on the deck, jammed up under the stern gunwale. Slovo's body was wedged beside her, the machete sticking through his torso and emerging out his back.

Chris pulled Slovo's body out of the way and helped Claudia to position herself more comfortably.

"I've got you, just hold on. I'm going back up to the helm. I'll be right back."

From somewhere nearby, Chris heard Mac yell, "Chris, you've got to get out of there!"

Chris felt the bottom drop out of his stomach as the boat dropped deep into the trough of a large wave. He looked up to see the crest of the wave begin to break over the side of the boat.

"Oh, crap."

The wave hit the boat hard from the side and it immediately began to go over. Chris had fractions of a second to recognize that the boat was not going to right itself this time. His last act before being pitched into the cold water was to grab hold of Claudia's wrist.

44

One evening around a bonfire on Carmel Beach back home, Chris had reflected on how quickly the brain processes information when under duress.

"What are you talking about?" Mac had asked.

"You must know what I'm talking about," Chris had replied. "Your experiences in battle must have invoked similar thoughts.

"When that white shark charged me down off Point Lobos, I saw my life flash before my eyes so clearly. It was as though I was watching it all pan out on screen. And it was not just vague details, cliché-type stuff. One second I was remembering exactly what it felt like to break my arm playing soccer that time back in middle school."

"Oh, yeah. I remember the guy that fell on you," Mac had interrupted. "The other coach had produced a birth certificate before the game to 'prove' the kid was age appropriate for the league. That was classic."

"The next second," Chris had continued, "I remembered how my stomach felt when I received my first question during my Ph.D. oral qualifying exam.

"The point is, there were many other considerations as well, and they all happened within seconds, or even fractions of seconds."

"That's pretty deep."

"Why do I hang out with you again?" Chris had laughed.

That distant conversation, and many others, now swirled around in Chris's head as he simultaneously tried to hold tight to Claudia's wrist, to determine where the boat was, and to figure out which way was up. He could feel Claudia struggling to find her way up too, which was a good sign. He was also encouraged when the shadow of the overturned boat passed over them, suggesting he didn't necessarily have to worry about that particular threat right at that instant.

Pulling Claudia with him, Chris kicked vigorously toward the light. Once at the surface he quickly pulled Claudia to him so he could support her head above the water line. They were now well within the breaking waves. The shock of the cold water kept him alert as he looked for Mac, but the frequent passage of breaking waves over his head continued to diminish his energy.

During a brief break in the swells Chris could hear the Whaler's engines approaching.

"Here!" Mac yelled as he approached, dangling his right arm over the side. Chris lifted Claudia as much as he could and was relieved to feel Mac grab hold of her and pull her up.

Relieved of having to support someone else, Chris took a few seconds to surveil the situation. He could see the overturned hull of the cabin cruiser washing closer to the rocks, which were surprisingly close at this point.

"Incoming!" Mac yelled.

Chris turned as the Whaler approached. Mac idled the engine and Chris reached up to pull himself up onto the boat. His fingers were not working well, but they weren't critical to getting him out of the water.

"Yo! There's a set coming, get yourself in so we can get out of here!"

With one final lunge, Chris pulled himself into the Whaler just as Mac gunned the engines and steamed directly into the next oncoming wave.

Once they were safely beyond the breaking waves, Mac turned the boat south to head back toward Hout Bay. With the waves coming in behind them now, the ride was significantly more comfortable.

Chris pulled out three life jackets to provide some support for Claudia. Her skin was turning gray, her lips blue. He used a small towel to keep pressure on her wound.

"You're a mess, Chris," Claudia said weakly.

"Yeah, I've been better. But you look great."

Claudia tried to laugh but winced at the pain in her side.

"What happened, Claudia?"

"Before we got in the boat, Slovo sliced the zip tie off my wrists."

"Why'd he do that?" Chris asked.

Claudia coughed and then responded slowly. "I'll get to that. Once we left the marina and rounded that bend, Slovo focused on fighting the swells. He was ignoring me, so I snuck down into the galley and found the emergency flare kit. I'd just made it out onto the back deck when he dropped from above and stabbed me with his machete. Somehow, I was able to fire off a flare."

The effort to talk had clearly exhausted her.

"Don't talk anymore. Help is on its way. Can you hear those sirens?" Chris adjusted his position so that he could maintain the pressure on her wound. He looked back toward Mac, who nodded in understanding and accelerated.

Claudia reached up. Though his arm was cold, her hand felt colder. "Chris, it was me. I was the leak. It was me."

"What are you talking about?"

"They have my brother. Greyling . . . he has Charlie. He's just a kid. They kidnapped him and made me provide information. I'm so, so sorry." She began crying.

"I wanted to tell you. Tried to tell you." Chris could tell that her breathing was becoming increasingly labored.

"Where do they have Charlie? Do you have any idea?"

"A farm. I don't know exactly where, but I don't think it's far outside of town. They let me visit once, but I was blindfolded." She grabbed Chris by his shirt and pulled him close as she whispered. "Charlie is all I have. I had to save him." She took a deep, painful breath. "Tell Charlie that I love him."

"Claudia, hold on. We'll get Charlie back. I promise."

". . . get Charlie . . . Chris . . . tell him . . ."

And then Claudia closed her eyes forever.

45

The "post mortem," a term Mac used to refer to debriefings, happened in stages. Stage one involved the authorities, including local police from the municipalities of Hout Bay and Nordhoek as well as the South African Police (SAPS) whose jurisdiction was national in scope.

The circumstances surrounding the deaths of Claudia, Slovo, and four men at the lookout were initially of great interest to local police. Chris and Mac, whose many plans had not included a coherent narrative about the bigger picture that would be digestible by local police, were prepared mentally to spend time behind bars. Preliminary interviews were conducted in the parking lot at the Hout Bay marina and, in Chris's estimation, did not go well.

"Dr. Black, can you explain how you came to be on the vessel with Claudia Schwarz and Jacob Slovo?"

"I was seeking to help Ms. Schwarz."

"You indicated in an earlier answer that Slovo had kidnapped Ms. Schwarz. Can you explain why he would want to do that?"

Chris paused, considering his answer carefully. "It's complicated."

"We have witnesses that place you at the scene of a shootout at the lookout point; a shootout that resulted in the deaths of four men. Can you explain what you were doing there?"

"That is even more complicated."

Chris had grown up with a deep respect for most of the people who worked in law enforcement. His most recent encounter with the police back in California had reinforced his belief that, like other professions and the rest of society, the authorities encompassed both the best and worst of humanity. He did not want to intentionally evade questions from the local police, but because the discrete questions that they were asking were part of a much larger continuous narrative, a narrative that involved sunken treasure, Chris was unclear how to proceed.

He was also reeling internally from the loss of Claudia and the revelation that she had been blackmailed to provide information to Greyling.

An intervention by officers from the SAPS ended the discussion with the local police. The two officers took custody of Chris and Mac and transported them back to a conference room at NAMARI. There they found Kathryn, Daniel, Mbeke, Kara, as well as Donagan and four other men who were not identified, in the midst of an animated discussion.

Chris and Mac were seated at the large round table in the center of the room. The two officers stood at the perimeter. Everyone else was seated, including someone who appeared to be documenting everything being said.

"Now, Dr. Black," Frank Donagan said, who'd adopted an overtly formal aspect as soon as Chris and Mac had entered to the room. "We've been discussing the broader context for the many shocking occurrences of the past several weeks. And we think that you might be able to help."

"I will do everything that I can."

"Thank you. I believe Ms. Wekesa has a question for you first."

Kathryn turned toward Chris. "Dr. Black, I would first like to thank you for your help in seeking the release of myself and my former colleague, Claudia Schwarz, from our abductors. I would also like to thank you for your assistance in the discovery of the gold found in the hold of the wreck located in the Ark Rock marine protected area."

Chris nodded.

"That said, your decision to remove the gold, however well intentioned, was a shocking violation of South African and maritime law with far reaching consequences that we are still working to understand. So, my question to you is this: how can you possibly justify that action?"

The rest of the room, Chris thought, was eerily silent. Exhaustion washed over him. None of the plans they'd made now seemed adequate to the task. They'd saved Kathryn, but they'd failed Claudia.

Claudia. He hadn't known her long enough, and she'd lied to him. But her death was horrible in its own way. She'd matched his sarcasm virtually word for word. He'd rarely experienced that outside of his close colleagues.

And now her younger brother was completely alone, and still a hostage.

And Greyling, the mastermind behind it all, though shot in the shoulder during the confrontation at the lookout point, had disappeared before anyone else had arrived on site. His whereabouts were unknown. Chris was not happy with himself for letting him get away. Things had just happened to quickly for him to chase after Slovo *and* take care of Greyling.

"Dr. Black?"

"I cannot," he said, looking toward Donagan and the two mysterious men seated to his left, and the two standing behind him against the wall.

"You cannot justify the decision to remove the gold?" Donagan asked.

"That is correct. I cannot justify that decision because I did not make it."

The mystery man sitting immediately adjacent to Donagan asked, "Are you suggesting that someone else made the decision to remove the gold?"

"No sir," Chris said. "I am stating that I cannot justify the decision to remove the gold because the gold was not removed. It remains, to the best of my knowledge, in the bow of the wreck as we found it." There were several surprised gasps around the table, with Kathryn Wekesa the most visibly surprised.

"Mac Johnson, seated here to my right, has high definition video documenting our discovery of the barrels, our efforts to determine what was in the barrels, and the condition of the wreck after we departed it. We will be happy to turn that video over to the appropriate recipient at any time."

"Then how can you explain the presence of the salvage vessel, *Queen of England*, on site at the wreck?" Kathryn asked.

"It is important to understand two things," Chris said. "First, it was clear to several of us as the tragic events unfolded that the criminals were receiving information from someone either working for NAMARI or someone closely associated with our efforts."

"And second, we were able to confirm my hypothesis that there were actually two wrecks within very close proximity to one another."

"How is that relevant?" Kathryn asked.

"I believe that the criminals never actually had direct contact with the gold-bearing wreck. We know that they received a copy of the high-resolution topographic map depicting a single wreck. My theory, which now seems to be supported by the facts, is that they erred in their initial exploration of the wreck by diving on the other wreck; a fishing boat of very similar dimensions. It is the second wreck that exploded, most likely due to some explosives they planted on it."

"And the salvage vessel?" the second mystery man sitting near Donagan asked.

"The salvage vessel had two objectives," Chris explained. "The first was to be seen on site. Given that we did not know who was providing information to the criminals, the presence of the salvage vessel would likely give the impression that something was being salvaged. Judging by the response of people in the room here, I'd say that impression was pretty compelling."

"And the second objective?"

"We had them place three orange surface buoys marking the second wreck as the focal point of activity before they departed. Our hope was that if any of the criminals returned to the general area, they would repeat their error of diving on the wrong wreck. But we wanted to make sure that was the case. After I implied that we had removed the gold they needed to see a wreck with no gold. And it appears that they did."

One of the men standing in the shadows stepped forward and asked what was to be the final question of the session. "Are you aware of any person in this room, or working for NAMARI, who provided the criminals with information?"

Chris paused for a moment and said, "I am not."

46

Chris and Mac were delivered back to Chris's rental flat and admonished not to leave the premises. They both promptly fell into exhausted sleep and consequently honored the admonishment for approximately twelve hours.

The next morning, when Chris extracted himself from bed and found his way to the kitchen, Hendrix was sitting at the table drinking a tea and reading a newspaper.

"Good morning, sunshine!" Hendrix said.

"I think that's my line," Chris replied.

"Well, it's a good one. You should spread it around. Where's Johnson?"

"Here," an obviously groggy Mac said as he stumbled into the kitchen and sat down.

"How did the inquisition go yesterday?" Hendrix asked.

"Your name came up frequently," Mac said. "There are number of important people who want to speak with you. Did you bring a tie with you to Africa?"

Hendrix shook his head wearily. "Can I take it as a good sign that neither of you is currently behind bars?"

Chris shrugged and Mac grunted. "We have been instructed not to leave the premises."

"That's a pity," Hendrix said, as he conspicuously folded his newspaper and set it down in front of him, attracting looks from both Chris and Mac.

"You found it?"

Hendrix nodded. "I did."

"Found what?" Mac asked.

"The farm is not far outside of town," Hendrix said, "near the Tygerberg Nature Reserve."

"I don't know where that is. How well guarded?" Chris asked.

"Not very. It appears that they are understaffed after the events at the lookout.".."

"Okay, I'm coming up to speed," Mac said before he asked, "Why didn't you just go and grab the kid?"

Hendrix took a sip of his tea and looked toward Chris. "Because I think Dr. Black would like to be involved in such an operation. Am I correct?"

"You are. Did you note any surveillance on your way in here?" Chris asked.

"Nothing that we can't evade with relative ease."

"Then it sounds like we're going," Mac said.

One hour later, Chris, Mac, and Hendrix were joined by four of Hendrix's men at a hillside location overlooking the farm. From that vantage point the farm appeared entirely normal. But the longer they watched they started to see the changing of the guards at various locations around the farm. Chris noted with interest that none of the other farms that he could see had armed men guarding them. "Why aren't the cops here? Even if we don't know where Greyling is, his organization is clearly no longer a secret."

Hendrix was on the phone with team members down closer to the farm. He pulled the phone away from his ear. "We know Greyling's been at this for a long time. The police are combing through the house where he was living. It's likely that he or others in his group have a number of properties. It will take the SAPS some time to track them all down."

He spoke a few more minutes before clicking off his phone and turning to Chris and Mac. "Here's how I recommend we play it."

Ten minutes later Chris and Mac drove straight up the long drive to the main building, a large single-story ranch house. No guards were visible out front from where they parked.

"I suppose now is not the time to point out that you and I don't have a great record with isolated houses far out in valleys." Chris knew Mac was referring to the *Carmel Canyon Incident*.

"The only question in my mind, is when you'll stop talking about it."

Knowing that snipers were covering them from places unknown, they left the car and walked up to the front door and knocked. To their mutual surprise, a small, grey-haired woman in a flower-print dress answered the door. Chris figured that very likely, there were women such as this at farms all over the world. He just didn't expect to see one at a farm so heavily guarded.

"Good afternoon, ma'am. We're here to pick up Charlie Schwarz."

"Of course, of course. We've been expecting someone," the woman said in a heavy Afrikaner accent. "Please come in."

Mac gave Chris a look he'd seen many times before; a look that said "we're not in Kansas anymore, Toto."

The woman led them down a long hallway. "Am I to understand that Master Greyling has been apprehended by the authorities?"

"Not as far as we know, ma'am." Chris looked toward Mac to see if this bizarre situation was hitting him in a similar way.

"Is that so?" She approached a closed door on the left. "Here we are. You will find Charlie in here."

"Excuse me, ma'am," Mac said. "Are there more people like Charlie here on this farm right now?"

"No, he is the last one. But please feel free to check for yourselves if you don't believe me." And with that, she returned the way she had come.

Chris knocked twice on the door and then opened it. He and Mac proceeded down a narrow passage, boarded to the right by a small bathroom and a closet. As they stepped out into the room, they encountered a blonde teenager sitting at a small desk below a narrow window positioned high up on the wall. He appeared to be studying and did not look up immediately.

Mac cleared his throat and the boy turned quickly.

"Oh! I thought you were one of the guards. Who are you?"

Chris wasn't sure about the best way to proceed, so he opted for the most direct. "My name's Chris and this is Mac. We're friends of Claudia."

"Are you Chris Black?" Charlie asked.

"I am. But how do you know that?"

"Claudia came out here once. She told me about you." He looked down and away. "I think she likes you, or something."

"Well, I like her, too. And she told me a lot about you. Would you like to come with us, Charlie? It's time to get you out of here."

"Yes! Just let me collect my things."

Hendrix's voice came in over Chris's earpiece. "Chris and Mac, be aware the situation has changed outside. Multiple armed guards now visible immediately outside the house. I'm not sure where they came from."

"Copy that," replied Mac, as he moved back down the short passage way toward the door.

"We'll take care of the situation outside," continued Hendrix. "But be aware that things in the house may not be what they appear."

"Charlie, we better get out of here," said Chris. He pulled a Kevlar vest from a pack on his back and handed it to Charlie. "Please put this on and come with us. We'll come back and get your stuff later, okay?"

Charlie's eyes bulged at the site of the vest. "Oh . . . okay."

From the door, Mac said, "Hallway is clear. But what do you think about that window?"

"Too narrow and too high up," replied Chris. "I think we have to try the hallway."

"Got it."

"Okay, Charlie. My friend Mac is going to lead the way down the hall. I want you to follow him. I'll be right behind you, okay?"

"Okay."

The far end of the hallway terminated at closed doors, so Mac led the trio back the way they had come, toward the front of the house. He was carrying a machine pistol in his hand. Chris had a similar weapon ready.

Just shy of the opening into the living room, Chris and Mac stopped to confer silently on a strategy to move out the front door. They were preparing to move when they heard an old, raspy voice. "Come on out Dr. Black. We've been waiting for you."

Chris recognized the voice.

"I don't think we'll do that just now, Mr. Greyling," Chris replied while motioning to Charlie to lie down on the floor.

"Suit yourself," said Greyling.

Two men leapt into view, both armed with automatic weapons. Mac shot both them before either had a chance to fire.

Greyling coughed. "Impressive. I expect that you're waiting for your commando friends outside to save you. We'll see about that."

As if on cue, huge explosions could be heard outside. The walls of the house shook, plaster dust rained down from the ceiling.

"Mines!" Mac yelled to Chris, and both of them dropped down to the floor, pulling Charlie down with them. Sheltering Charlie behind them, they were lying prone with their weapons pointed toward the living room.

Two more men came into view. Unlike their predecessors, they started shooting immediately, spraying bullets along both walls where Chris, Mac and Charlie had just been standing.

This time Chris shot one, and Mac the other.

"Got any more guys?" Chris yelled.

"Oh, yes, but they won't be necessary."

An explosion rocked the hallway behind them. Chris turned to see flames pour out of a doorway thirty feet beyond their position. Seconds later another explosion was triggered, and then a third, each new explosion moving progressively closer to Chris, Mac and Charlie.

"This is not looking good," Mac observed.

"No, it isn't," said Chris. "Hendrix. What's your status?"

Hendrix did not respond.

"Why aren't we already dead?" Mac whispered.

Chris couldn't answer that.

Two more explosions rocked the hallway, the second close enough to rain debris down on the threesome.

Chris's ears buzzed in the aftermath of the last explosion, but he could still hear Greyling say, "Dr. Black, the next explosion will not go well for you unless you step out of the hallway."

Chris and Mac shared a glance. There had been no communication from Hendrix since the fighting had begun outside. They would very likely not survive exposure to Greyling and his goons in the living room, but there was no chance they'd survive the next blast in the hallway.

Leaning close to Mac, Chris whispered, "I say we give up. Maybe we can save Charlie that way."

"Not a great plan," responded Mac. "But I don't see any other way."

"Okay, we're coming out!"

Chris nodded to Charlie, then lead the way, holding his arms up. As he stepped into the living room, he could see Greyling, his arm in a sling, standing behind a couch, straddled on either side by heavily armed men.

"You're not looking too good, Greyling," observed Chris as he held one arm up while with the other he pushed Charlie behind him, shielding him with bis body.

"Yeah, you're kind of grey around the eyes," added Mac, also stepping in front of the boy. "Now that's irony for you."

"Jovial American courage in the face of certain death," said Greyling, his raspy voice barely audible above din of fighting still being waged outside. "I've seen it before, and it won't last. Get on your knees."

Before Chris, Mac and Charlie could comply, the front door opened, revealing three of Greyling's paramilitary guards dressed in full regalia, including helmets with tinted face masks.

Greyling, temporarily distracted, smiled, revealing blackened teeth. "Good, you're just in time. I trust the situation outside is under control?"

The lead guard nodded.

"Excellent. Put these two men on their knees, and take the kid outside to my vehicle," commanded Greyling.

Two of the guards grabbed Charlie and virtually lifted him off his feet as they swept him out the front door. The remaining guard stepped behind Chris and Mac.

A calm descended over Chris as he faced the inevitable. The last few weeks, indeed the last year, had felt to him like a runaway train. Events had been speeding out of control constantly and they had barely survived each successively more violent encounter. Though he and Mac, often joined by Hendrix, joked from time to time about 'cheating death,' they largely avoided the subject in any earnest conversation.

Chris assumed that Mac and Hendrix, as combat soldiers, had resigned themselves to an early death years before. Chris did not fear death. He had spent much of his life avoiding it in as many ways as he could conjure, but it didn't scare him. In fact, since his father's passing several years before at a relatively early age of sixty-four, Chris had not been able to envision his own life lasting beyond his early sixties. While he could see many aspects of his future in his mind, living beyond his father's age was not one of them.

"I said, on your knees!" yelled Greyling.

When neither Chris nor Mac complied, the guard struck them both at their lower backs with the barrel of his automatic rifle. It had the intended effect.

Kneeling in front of the guard, and looking up at Willem Greyling, Chris asked, "What are you going to do with the kid?"

Greyling appeared caught off guard by the question. "He is young, and our cause can always use new recruits."

"Your cause? Are you planning to bring back Apartheid?"

Greyling laughed, which caused a coughing fit. When he finally recovered, he wiped bloody spittle from his mouth on a handkerchief. "There is no need to bring it back. Apartheid has never left. It is only a matter of funding a few key political efforts, and we will take back control. Not that you or any of your team will be here to see it."

"Well, Greyling, looking at you, it's pretty clear you won't be here either," Chris said, the satisfaction in his voice palpable.

"Yeah, and we'll be waiting for you," Mac added. "You can look forward to an eternity of getting your ass kicked every single day."

"Do it!" Greyling ordered.

The guard raised his rifle and pointed it at Chris's head.

Chris could feel the guard's movement behind him, and he was about to lunge backward in the hopes of giving Mac a slight chance at an escape, when the guard lifted the rifle higher and shot each of Greyling's two remaining henchmen in the face.

The guard then pointed the rifle at Greyling, who raised his one functional arm up in protest as he yelled, "No!"

A single shot rang out, striking Greyling in his right shoulder and knocking him onto his back.

Chris and Mac turned in unison to look up at the guard.

Hendrix removed his helmet. "Sorry it took me so long."

47

A week of house arrest passed. And as Mac noted on multiple occasions during that week, it became a real house arrest once it had been discovered that they had dodged surveillance in order to rescue Charlie Schwarz. They'd already taxed the South African authorities' patience, and the raid on the farm had "pushed them over the edge." Even Greyling's capture had not mollified the authorities.

Chris spent his time in a quiet depression for the first three days, unable to get out of a funk. But on day four he'd come upon a strategy that made him feel much better.

He talked to Karen Lee about engaging Charlie in her research at the university, and she was excited to do so. But then he'd come upon an even more satisfying solution. A call to Peter Lloyd back in Monterey had borne fruit—it took Peter just two days to arrange for Charlie's admission to the university's marine science program. A follow-up call with Kathryn, whose frustration with Chris had run its course, secured NAMARI funding for Charlie's education in the U.S. Chris hoped he could honor Claudia's memory by facilitating her brother's scientific training.

On day seven, Chris answered a knock at the door to find Frank Donagan standing on the doorstep. He wore the same sunglasses and the same expression as the first day Chris met him.

"Good morning, Dr. Black!"

"Good morning, Frank."

"I come bearing good tidings. May I come in?"

"Please do."

Mac, who was sitting on the couch, looked up. "What exactly are 'good tidings?'"

The answer, Chris noted, rolled off Frank's tongue about as quickly as he expected. "Good question, Mr. Johnson! It is generally considered to mean 'good news.' Some think it derives from the Old English word 'tidan,' which means 'to happen.'"

"Speaking of that," Chris interjected, "What is happening?"

"Well the occasion you've asked me about so many times has finally arrived."

Mac looked quizzical. It took Chris a couple of beats to understand what Frank was talking about. "You mean I'm being kicked out of the country?"

"Not technically, but one could make the argument that the effect is the same. Your six-month work visa has been cancelled. Mac is just here on a ninety-day tourist visa, so he is just being strongly encouraged to join you on this evening's flight back to the States."

"We're leaving tonight? That soon?" He looked around at the gear strewn around the flat.

Donagan replied, "Indeed. One shouldn't dillydally in these situations."

"What does dillydallying actually mean?" Mac asked. "Is that even a legit word?"

"Oh yes, it's a verb meaning 'to waste time through aimless wandering or indecision,' which is something we must not do!"

"What about you, Frank? Are you seeing any impact from your role in this affair?" Mac asked.

"Let's just say that none of us, with the possible exception of Hendrix, has come out of this completely clean. Kathryn Wekesa's leadership of

NAMARI will be scrutinized for some time to come, at least until they determine who was providing information to Greyling and Slovo. Are you sure you don't know anything about that?"

Chris shrugged. "You mean beyond de Klerk?"

"Right," Donagan said. "The full extent of what de Klerk did probably died with him because Greyling isn't talking. That guy is 'old school' tough. He'll easily never see the outside of a cell again, but he will say nothing to make his incarceration more palatable."

Donagan arched his eyebrows and cast a probing glance at Chris. "People are asking questions about Claudia Schwarz, too. Some people seem to think that her brother was held captive in order to blackmail her. But there is no hard evidence of this yet or of anything she might have told them."

Chris returned the stare, his face impassive.

"Fine. By the way, back on de Klerk. I read the transcript from the interrogation of the two guys Hendrix's men captured here last week. De Klerk died a horrible, horrible death. He apparently only realized the full magnitude of his situation immediately before he was tossed overboard to the sharks. And then he was literally split in half within the first two minutes in the water."

Mac shuddered.

"If there were real justice," Donagan continued, "That would be Greyling's fate, as well. But obviously I don't get to make those decisions. So now all we can hope for is that some inmates take issue with his Apartheid-era activities."

"What about the NAMARI rank and file?" Mac asked. "People like Daniel, Mbeke, and Kara?"

"I'm not sure about Daniel," Donagan replied. "I know Chris thinks he's in the clear, but there will still be some tough questions for Daniel in the coming weeks.

"Mbeke and Kara should be fine. They didn't know enough to be the source of the leaks, and their youthful earnestness is endearing."

"What's going to happen with the gold?" Chris asked.

Donagan smiled. "You'll likely be happy to learn that the *Queen of England* will actually be engaged to recover the gold."

"No one said the government had to be creative," Mac said. "If our plan can help them out, great. But make sure they know it was our plan."

"Oh, I won't be around to do that," Donagan said.

"You're leaving, as well?" Chris asked.

"Not tonight. But my days in country are numbered. You'll probably be able to come visit me at the North Pole office sometime soon. I hear we have great views."

Frank stayed with Chris and Mac until their gear was packed and loaded into the waiting van. He joked most of the time, but it was clear to Chris that one of Donagan's remaining tasks in his current position was to get Chris and Mac out of the country.

"Listen, Frank," Chris said.

"I'm listening, but I'm already feeling a headache coming on."

"We need to make one stop on the way to the airport."

48

The cemetery where Claudia Schwarz's remains were interred was not on the way to the airport, but Donagan and his team obliged Chris this final request before he got on the plane.

The Pinelands 2 Jewish Cemetery was near the University of Cape Town. It looked to Chris very much like a cemetery should look, with grass, trees, and headstones in appropriate proportions. He left Mac and Donagan standing by the vehicles as he walked over the fresh grave marking Claudia's remains.

Chris struggled with the appropriate emotion for the moment, knowing that Margaret would tell him any emotion is appropriate if it was what he was feeling. So what was he feeling? Conflicted, not at all resolved. She had come on strong, and he'd felt a clear connection to her. Claudia's sense of humor had been compelling and her frankness refreshing. But then, of course, she'd used him, taken advantage of him, lied to him.

Chris's internal dialogue couldn't reach consensus on that last point. Yes, Claudia had lied. And she had contributed to the deaths of many people as a result of her complicity. But she was also motivated by her love for her brother, the one remaining relative she had. Recalling how sarcastic and funny Claudia had been, and how quickly she had felt comfortable sharing that with him, Chris felt profound sadness welling up in his chest.

Sensing that this quandary would go unresolved for some time, Chris opted for the only closure he could get at the moment. He knelt down in front of Claudia's headstone, which was still adorned with flowers and notes from mourners, and placed his hand on the brand new headstone. His eyes closed, he nonetheless could feel the approach of someone from his right. As he slowly stood, without looking, he could tell it was Mac.

Mac placed his hand on Chris's shoulder. "Donagan says we have to leave. He didn't want to be insensitive, so he sent me."

"Okay."

The two stood silently for several minutes. Nothing needed to be said. "I've known Mac for three decades," Chris had explained to Claudia back on the ship. "We don't have to say much anymore. We *know*."

"What do you know?" Claudia had asked.

"We know when to joke, and when to stay quiet. We know when to fight, and when to run. We know what matters."

Claudia had been quiet for several moments. Then she'd nodded. "You are incredibly fortunate to have him. And he, you."

"Yeah. Well, sometimes I still want to kill him."

"Well, sure. I've only known you for two weeks and I want to kill you sometimes." They'd both laughed at that, so much so that someone in the adjoining stateroom had pounded on the wall.

Smiling again at that memory, Chris looked at Mac. "The awful spirits of the deep, hold their communion there; And there are those for whom we weep, the young, the bright, the fair."

"Is that Shakespeare?" Mac asked.

"No, it's from a poem called *The Ocean*, by Nathaniel Hawthorne."

"Do you remember the rest?"

Chris dredged the depths of his memory briefly and then said,

The Ocean has its silent caves,
Deep, quiet, and alone;
Though there be fury on the waves,
Beneath them there is none.

The awful spirits of the deep
Hold their communion there;
And there are those for whom we weep,
The young, the bright, the fair.

Calmly the wearied seamen rest
Beneath their own blue sea.
The ocean solitudes are blest,
For there is purity.

The earth has guilt, the earth has care,
Unquiet are its graves;
But peaceful sleep is ever there,
Beneath the dark blue waves.

"This isn't an easy one to process, is it?" Mac asked.

"No, it isn't," Chris replied.

"I guess none of them ever are. I'm not sure I would have made the same choices she made."

"I know. But then, I've not been faced with that particular challenge. I think she did what she felt she had to do. Can we ask more of anyone?"

49

Pulling up outside the terminal at Cape Town International Airport, the utter chaos of a busy terminal instantly engulfed them. Standing on the curb and speaking above the steady roar of people and vehicles, Donagan promised his services should they ever need them.

"Am I ever going to need them?" Chris hoped that he would not but knew that given his recent track record, it was a likely necessity at some point.

"Oh, I should think so," Frank answered. "I think we'll meet again. And I look forward to it."

"No *Parthian shot*?" Mac asked.

"Not bad Mr. Johnson. Not bad. Keep working on it, and we'll see how you've improved when we meet again. And have a nice flight."

Chris and Mac were escorted all the way to the gate by two unenthusiastic employees of the U.S. Embassy. Both of the men sported military haircuts and ear pieces, and neither said anything. The obvious and immediate benefit of this escort was their ability to bypass the queue at security, which was longer than either Chris or Mac had ever seen.

"How long have you guys been working in country?" Mac asked as the gate came into view above the masses.

There was no response from either man.

"Hmmm, I guess the answer is too long," Mac continued. "What would happen if we don't get on the plane?"

At that, the taller of the two men responded, "I don't recommend that."

"You don't recommend it. But you're not saying we can't do it. Are you?"

The second man then joined in, "Tell Hendrix that he owes us one."

"Why?" Mac asked.

They approached the gate, with another long queue already formed. The taller agent flashed an ID to the gate attendant, and Chris and Mac were inserted at the front of the line.

"Thanks so much!" Mac waved at the departing agents. Chris noted that most of the people in line were actively wondering what was going on with these two guys.

Working their way back to the rear of the plane, having arrived at the gate as the last group number was being called, Mac noted with some frustration that the thirteen-hour flight to Heathrow in London was a long time to fly in coach. His mood did not improve when they passed Hendrix, who was reclining in what appeared to Chris to be a very comfortable bed-seat in first class. He was talking to an attractive dark-haired woman in the adjacent seat.

"I say, hello gents!" Hendrix affected a British accent. "Can I introduce you to Ms. Cornwallis?"

It wasn't until a couple of hours into the flight that Chris observed any improvement in Mac's attitude. When he returned from a trip to the bathroom with a smile on his face, Chris asked, "Do I dare ask what's up?"

"It's possible, just possible, that I may have accidentally spilled ice water onto Hendrix's bed-seat up there. This dry coach seat isn't looking so bad now!"

Chris chuckled and resumed looking out the window at the immense darkness below. They were flying directly north across the long axis of the continent, and there was literally not a light as far as Chris could see.

A little later, after watching parts of what Chris estimated to be three separate movies, Mac asked, "So where to next, boss?"

Chris replied, "I hadn't given it much thought. It's just a pleasure to serve."

"Sure, sure. Yadda, yadda, yadda. So, I ask again, where are we going next?"

"I'm just looking forward to being home, playing with Thig, and relaxing a bit."

Holding his right index finger up to keep Mac from asking a third time, he added, "But, but . . . *if* there were to be a next trip on the horizon, I'd recommend that you start reviewing your Darwin and practicing your Spanish."

That seemed to satisfy Mac, who then booted up another romantic comedy and reclined his seat.

Acknowledgments

Blood Cold would not have seen the light of day were it not for the generous contribution of time and constructive suggestions from Jeb Thornburg, Andrew DeVogelaere, Carrie Bretz, and Nancy Lindholm. I would also like to thank CamCat Publishing for supporting a re-release of this Chris Black adventure, and Dr. Helga Schier in particular for her excellent editorial insights.

This is obviously a work of fiction, but much of the world inhabited by Chris Black and his team is based in fact. Though (thankfully) most scientists don't have to deal with violent bad guys while conducting their field research, they do have to grapple with challenging environmental conditions and the implications of a constantly changing political landscape. Though a little license is taken here and there, the use of SCUBA in the story is accurate, as is the use of one-person submersibles. Marine Protected Areas (MPAs) are now common in most coastal countries in the world.

For the record, Cape Town, South Africa, is an extraordinary place to visit and should occupy a high ranking on every reader's bucket list. In particular, I strongly encourage intrepid travelers to arrange a pre-dawn trip out to Seal Island in False Bay. After reading the first chapter you'll know why. Also not-to-be-missed are trips down to the Cape of Good Hope (beware the baboons), up to Table Mountain (beware of heights), and to the Kirstenbosch Botanical Garden (beware of . . . well, you'll see), where Chris Black eats dinner early in the story.

For Further Discussion

1. What do you know about the Apartheid Era in South Africa? And how have things changed on the ground in the years since the end of Apartheid?
2. It is not unusual for members of failed regimes like Apartheid to continue to exert influence years following the end of a regime. Can you think of any other prominent examples in history?
3. What do you know about the impact of totalitarian regimes on environmental conservation? Look it up, you may be surprised.
4. White sharks *(Carcharodon carcharias)* feature prominently in the story. Beyond their cinematic roles (e.g., *Jaws* or *47 Meters Down*) what do you know about white sharks?
5. The Center for Marine Exploration (CMEx), where Chris Black works in Monterey, California, and National Marine Research Institute (NAMARI) where he works when he's in South Africa, are both fictional. What do you know about research institutes dedicated to studying the ocean? Where is the closets such institution to your residence?
6. Chris Black faces a number of challenging situations in the story. What is your assessment of the choices he made? And what, if anything, would you have done differently?

About the Author

Dr. James Lindholm is an author who dives deep for his inspiration. His novels stem from a foundation of direct, personal experience with the undersea world. He has lived underwater for multiple 10-day missions to the world's only undersea laboratory and has found himself alone on the seafloor staring into the eyes of a hungry great white shark. He has drafted text for an executive order for the White House and has briefed members of the House and Senate on issues of marine science and policy. James Lindholm's diverse writing portfolio includes textbooks, peer-reviewed scientific journal articles, and action/adventure novels.

For more information, please visit www.jameslindholm.com.

An Excerpt from *Dead Men's Silence*,

Chris Black's Third Adventure

1

Damien Wood died first. In the dwindling twilight of a Colombian sunset, a pirate cut his throat from ear to ear as he sat at the helm of his father's sixty-foot cabin cruiser *Innovator*. The entire incident took less than twenty seconds. One instant he was leisurely staring out the cruiser's front wind shield, smiling as he thought about the last *Game of Thrones* episode he'd watched; the next, he was dying. Damien's last conscious act was to look down at the blood pouring over his tanned-but-skinny torso and wonder, "What the hell?"

The *Innovator* had left Newport Beach two months prior and slowly worked its way down the length of Baja California and along the Mexican mainland in four weeks' time. Investment banker Jared Wood had been initially hesitant to loan out the *Innovator* to his son Damian and his friends. He'd only owned the boat for a year at that point and had hardly had any time to spend on it himself.

Wood had ordered the crew, via satellite phone, to steer clear of Honduras, El Salvador, and Nicaragua for fear that they might run afoul of "bad people." But it was at the last stop the *Innovator* made in Colombia that the boat had caught the attention of four men lurking in a small converted fishing boat at the perimeter of the partying crowd. The five crew of the *Langosta Espinosa* were nondescript enough to move freely among the boats moored around the island without attracting attention. The boat itself was unremarkable, and the five Hispanic males that operated it could have fit in anywhere along the Central American coast.

If anyone had looked closely, they would have seen that the wooden hulled boat had clearly not been doing any actual lobster fishing for some time; with traps irreparably broken and fouled on the back in a way no active fishermen would ever allow. But in a crowd more concerned with merriment than potential dangers, no one gave the boat or the crew a second look. And the lagging Colombian economy had left the already under-funded coast guard with very few assets to patrol the extensive coastline.

Late in the morning the *Innovator* had crossed into Colombian waters and sought refuge in the first cove the captain could find. The last week of partying had taken its toll on all passengers aboard, and the group required rest. As life-long, unrepentant nerds, Damien and his friend Stephen Long had survived this far with minimal experience at this type of alcohol-fueled merriment. Damien's other friend, Mike Hanson, had done his share of partying during his football days, but he'd not done so in years. As such, though all three guys had warmed quickly to the opportunities for celebration among their international boating community, they'd not had much endurance.

Further, cracks had begun to form in the façade holding the three young men together. Though as roommates during freshman and sophomore years at the University of Southern California, Damien and Mike had quickly worked out the challenges of living in close quarters together, Stephen had no such training. He'd lived at home in his parent's basement for what little of college he'd attended before departing USC for the glory of movie business. By the time the *Innovator* had reached Colombia, Stephen was complaining more frequently about Mike's nightly snoring. Mike, in turn, noted that Stephen rarely cleaned up after himself, leaving "his shit all over the place" while he played games on his smart phone. Damien had simply been frustrated by how stupid he'd thought these complaints were as he tried to keep the peace.

As the *Innovator*'s first day in Colombian waters came to a close, the three friends were as far apart from each other as the boat allowed, each lost in his own thoughts. That made them easy targets.

After Damian, Stephen Long died next; and just as quickly. He was stretched out on the *Innovator*'s bow playing a driving game called *Asphalt 8* on his smart phone. Stephen was so immersed in the game that he didn't sense the pirate's presence until his attention was redirected to the handle of the eight-inch ka-bar knife sticking out of his chest.

Damien's friend since middle school, Stephen had dropped out of the USC's film program two years prior to launch his career in the movies. Unfortunately for Stephen, his recently launched career as third assistant to the director had lasted approximately six months. The film he'd quit school to work on was cancelled mid-production due to the producers' financial issues.

For every pound that Damien had been missing from his torso, Stephen had made up for it on his own. He looked down at his chubbiness for the last time and wondered where his mom and dad were. *Asphalt 8* continued on its own for another two minutes until the phone's battery went as dead as Stephen.

Mike Hanson put up a fight. He was down in the galley making his second sandwich for the evening, when the third pirate came through the main hatch to get to him. At six foot four inches and two-hundred and fifty pounds, Mike looked at the smaller man wielding a knife and smiled.

Mike decided to resolve the situation quickly in his favor. Growing up in south central Los Angeles as the only child of a single, African-

American mother, Mike had learned early to solve problems before they came back to 'bite him in the ass.' He grabbed the wooden cutting board on which his second sandwich rested and struck at the pirate, crushing the man's nose with one strike. Mike then retracted the board and quickly struck again at the pirate's wind pipe, forcing a guttural cough from the man as he collapsed.

Satisfied that he'd ended the incident, Mike paused to listen for other trouble. Hearing no immediate threats, he leaned over to pick up the pirate's knife, thinking he'd better check on his two less physically capable friends right away. The pirate could have already attacked one of them before coming down to the galley, he thought.

Rising back to nearly his full height, slumping slightly so his head didn't hit the galley ceiling, Mike heard a metallic click that he didn't recognize. Before he had a moment to consider it further, a gunshot from the fourth pirate hit him in his left shoulder.

The impact of the bullet spun Mike around so he was now facing the pirate who'd just shot him. Neither of them moved as the gun's loud report still wrung in their ears.

Mike glanced down at the wound on his shoulder, and then peered through narrowed eyes at the pirate. As the man raised his weapon again, Mike used the cutting board, which was still in this right hand, to swipe upward, across his body. The force of the blow dislodged the gun from the pirate's hand and broke the cutting board in half.

Not waiting to give the pirate another chance, Mike hurled his large body up the steps toward the back deck. "Damien! Watch out—." His warning caught in his throat as he found Damien's body slumped in the chair at the helm, a gaping hole where his neck used to be and his chest covered in blood.

Grabbing his own bleeding shoulder, Mike stepped around the edge of the wheelhouse and moved as quickly as the narrow walkway would allow toward the bow. The shock of seeing his friend dead was briefly tempered by the adrenaline surging through his body. Perhaps if he could get to Stephen in time, they could both escape together.

He could hear someone coming behind him, but before he could turn around, Mike had arrived at the portion of the walkway that opened onto the *Innovator's* bow, revealing Stephen's lifeless body lying against a hatch. "Oh, my god."

Briefly stymied by the realization that his friends were no longer with him, Mike hesitated. In that moment a pirate appeared around the edge of the wheelhouse. The man expertly tossed a large knife in the air, caught it by the blade, and then threw it directly at Mike's chest.

Mike frantically deflected the knife with his right forearm, the blade slicing deeply into his muscle before dropping to the deck and sliding over the side.

Now nursing two wounds, Mike determined that his best course of action in the increasing darkness was to flee. He grabbed the rail with his bloodied right hand and launched himself over the side.

Plunging deep into the warm Pacific water, Mike surfaced away from the *Innovator* and began stroking toward the shore, leaving blood in his wake. He could see lights shimmering at multiple spots along the edge of the large cove from what he hoped were houses or hotels. Someone there would be able to help him.

It was a long swim for Mike, at least the length of a football field. He was not a natural swimmer, and with both arms impeded by injuries, his progress was slow. Approximately halfway to shore, he heard what he thought was the sound of a small outboard motor. Pausing to listen over his labored breathing, it sounded to Mike as though the small boat was headed away from him. Maybe this plan was going to work.

Struggling with declining mobility in his limbs and significant blood loss, Mike continued to make progress toward land. He could see the silhouetted shapes of people walking along the shore, but he was too tired to produce a coherent cry for help. Pausing again to catch his breath, new hope swelled in Mike as his feet drifted down to touch the sandy bottom below. He'd made it!

His feet touching the bottom, he could now use both his legs and arms to make progress toward shore, which he began to do with great effort. Exhausted and delirious, Mike failed to process the tugging he sensed down by his right leg. When it persisted, he started to wonder if he'd become tangled in something.

Reaching down to remove whatever was holding him back, Mike was briefly shocked back into lucidity by the realization that his right leg was gone below his mid-thigh. His hand brushed against the end of what must have been his femur, surrounded by strands of tissue dangling in the water.

"What the f—?" exclaimed Mike, just before he was pulled underwater. He could feel the rough skin of the shark's nose on the underside of his right arm as it clenched its jaws around his torso.

Seconds after the attack began, it was over.

Twelve minutes later the *Innovator* was once again underway, this time alongside the *Langosta Espinosa*. Neither the simultaneous departure of the two vessels nor Mike's struggle for survival had registered among the partying crowd in nearby boats or along the shore. As the boats disappeared over the horizon, the bodies of Damien and Stephen joined Mike one last time as the pirates tossed them over the side, wrapped in an old fish net and anchored down by the dive weights that Jared Wood would never have the chance to use.

WHEN PIRATES ASK FOR RANSOM, CHRIS BLACK ANSWERS.

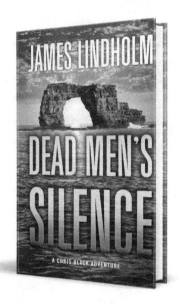

En route to the Galapagos Islands for a deep-sea diving trip with a group of international college students under his care, marine biologist Chris Black leaves his research vessel for a single night to enjoy dinner with friends. When he returns, the ship has vanished. With crew and passengers on board. Modern-day pirates hijacked the boat, hoping to collect a lucrative ransom. Amidst the storm of the century, indomitable Chris Black chases the pirates from island to island, fighting back to save the students under his care in a battle royal aboard the pirates' mysterious flagship.

Available now wherever books are sold.

CamCat Books

Visit Us Online for More Books to Live In:
camcatbooks.com

Follow Us:

CamCatBooks   @CamCatBooks   @CamCatBooks

CPSIA information can be obtained
at www.ICGtesting.com
Printed in the USA
BVHW061536010920
587791BV00002B/61